DROP-DEAD GORGEOUS

I watched.

Watched her swing that body around, shaking those breasts from side to side, always in perfect time to that awful music. Watched as she displayed herself, giving everybody a much longer look than they needed . . .

And heard her sudden gasp.

And saw the bead of blood on her left breast . . . watched her hands, moving in awful slow motion . . .

And watched her fall, still in slow motion, falling backwards and to her left, falling as only dead things fall, landing at last on the floorboards of the stage with the impact of a gunshot.

THE TOPLESS TULIP CAPER

THE TOPLESS TULIP CAPER

A CHIP HARRISON NOVEL

Lawrence Block

Ø

A SIGNET BOOK

SIGNET
Published by the Penguin Group
Penguin Putnam Inc., 375 Hudson Street,
New York, New York 10014, U.S.A.
Penguin Books Ltd, 27 Wrights Lane,
London W8 5TZ, England
Penguin Books Australia Ltd, Ringwood,
Victoria, Australia
Penguin Books Canada Ltd, 10 Alcorn Avenue,
Toronto, Ontario, Canada M4V 3B2
Penguin Books (N.Z.) Ltd, 182–190 Wairau Road,
Auckland 10, New Zealand

Penguin Books Ltd, Registered Offices:
Harmondsworth, Middlesex, England

Published by Signet, an imprint of Dutton Signet,
a member of Penguin Putnam Inc.
Originally published under the pseudonym Chip Harrison.

First Signet Printing, April, 1998
10 9 8 7 6 5 4 3 2 1

One

As I STARTED through the door a man stepped in front of me and stood there like the front four of the Miami Dolphins. I was about six inches taller than him, and he was about forty pounds heavier than I was, and I figured that gave him quite an edge. He was wearing plaid pants and a striped jacket over a sky-blue silk shirt. He had the face of an ex-boxer who had put on a lot of weight without going to fat. His nose had been broken more than once, and his eyes said he was just waiting for someone to try breaking it again. Someone very well might, sooner or later, because people usually get what they want, but I wasn't going to oblige him.

He said, "Read the sign, kid."

There were a lot of signs, so I started reading them aloud. " 'Treasure Chest,' " I said. " 'Girls! Girls! Girls!

'Topless Stopless Dancing!' 'Come in and see what Fun City is all about!' "

"You read nice," he said.

"Thanks."

"What you call reading with expression," he said. He took a step closer to me. "That particular sign," he said, pointing. "Let's see you read that one."

" 'You must be twenty-one and prove it,' " I intoned.

"Beautiful," he said. "Nice phrasing," he said. "Now get the fuck out of here," he said.

"I'm twenty-one," I lied.

"Sure you are, kid."

"Twenty-two, actually," I embroidered.

"Sure. You wanna try proving it?"

I took my wallet from the inside breast pocket of the sport jacket it was too damned hot to be wearing, and from the wallet I took a green rectangle with Alexander Hamilton's picture on it. I folded the piece of paper in half and put it carefully into his paw.

"My I.D.," I said.

His eyes grew very thoughtful. Actually, you don't have to be twenty-one to drink in New York. You have to be eighteen, which is something I can be with no problem whatsoever. But you have to be twenty-one to go into a place where ladies flash various portions of their anatomy at you. This is rarely a problem for me since I don't generally bother with that kind of place. Not because it does nothing for me to look at ladies with no clothes on, but because it does. I mean, I also don't go browsing in French restaurants when I don't have the price of a meal in my pocket. Why torture yourself, for Pete's sake?

But this was business. Leo Haig had a case and a client, and his client was performing at the Treasure Chest, and since Leo Haig was no more likely to hie himself off to a topless club than I was to enter a monastery, I, Chip Harrison, was elected to serve as Haig's eyes, ears, nose, and throat.

Which explains why I had just tucked a ten-dollar bill into a very large and callused hand.

"Ten bucks?" said the owner of the hand. "For ten bucks you could go to a massage parlor and get a fancy hand job."

"I'm allergic to hand lotion."

"Huh?"

"I get this horrible rash."

He frowned at me, evidently suspecting I was joking with him. He had a ready wit, all right. "Yeah," he said. "Well, I guess you just proved your age to the satisfaction of the management. One-drink minimum at the bar. Enjoy yourself, tell your friends what a good time you had."

He stepped aside and I moved past him. At least it was cooler inside. The Treasure Chest was located on Seventh Avenue between Forty-Eight and Forty-Ninth, a block which is basically devoted to porno movies and dirty bookstores and peep shows, but they didn't account for the temperature outside all by themselves. What accounted for it was that it was August and it hadn't rained in weeks and some perverse deity had taken a huge vacuum cleaner and sucked all the air out of Manhattan, leaving nothing behind but soot and sulphur dioxide and carbon monoxide and all the other goodies that only rats and pigeons and cockroaches can breathe with impunity. The sun was out there every day, having a fine old time, and when night finally came it didn't do much good because the buildings just grabbed onto the heat and held it in place until the sun could come up again and start the whole process over. It had been a sensational couple of weeks, let me tell you. Haig's place was air-conditioned, which was nice during the day, but my furnished room two blocks away was not. This made the nights terrible, and it also made it increasingly difficult for me to resist Haig's suggestion that I give up my room and move into his quarters.

"Archie Goodwin lives with Nero Wolfe," Haig said, more than once. "He is a ladies' man in every sense of the word. His cohabitation with Wolfe does not seem to inhibit his pursuit of the fair sex."

There were a lot of answers to this one. Such as mentioning that Wolfe had a brownstone to himself, while Haig had the top two floors of a carriage house in Chelsea, and you can't very well bring home an innocent young thing to the top two floors of a place the bottom two floors of which are occupied by Madam Juana's Puerto Rican cathouse. But what it came down to was that I liked having my own room in my own building, and that I could be very stubborn on the subject, almost as stubborn as Leo Haig himself.

But this is all beside the point, the point being that it was cooler inside the Treasure Chest. There wasn't much more to be said for the place, however. It was dimly lit, which worked to its advantage; what I could see of the furnishings suggested that they were better off the less you could make them out. There was a long bar on the left side as you entered, and behind the bar there was a stage, and on the stage, dancing in the glare of a baby spotlight, was our client, the one and probably only Tulip Willing.

She didn't have any clothes on.

I wasn't prepared for this. I mean, I should have been, and everything, but I somehow wasn't. I had seen Tulip that afternoon and what she'd been wearing then had made her figure overwhelmingly obvious to me. Tight jeans and a tight tee-shirt, both worn over nothing but skin, don't leave you very much up in the air as to what's going on underneath them. And also when you go into a topless-bottomless place you ought to be prepared to be confronted by some skin. That's what people go there for, for Pete's sake. Not because the drinks are terrific.

If it had been somebody else up there I think I could have handled it better. But I'd spent a few hours with Tulip, first at Haig's place and then at her apartment, and I had gotten to know her as a human being, and at the same time I had become enormously turned on by her personally, and there she was up there, twisting her unbelievable body around to a barrage of loud recorded hard rock, swinging her breasts and bumping her behind and strutting around on those long legs that seemed to go all the way up to her neck, and—

Well, you get the picture.

I took a deep breath of air that was probably just as polluted as all the other air but seemed better because it was several degrees cooler. I held the breath for a while, looking at Tulip, surveying the club, then looking at Tulip again. She looked a lot better than the club. I let the breath out and walked over to the bar. There were two empty stools and I took the closest one. I had the other empty stool on my right, and on my left I had a man wearing a dark three-button suit and an expression of rapt adoration. I wouldn't say that his eyes were on stems exactly, but they weren't as far back in his head as most people's are, either. He looked as though he'd leaped out of a fairy tale, trapped forever halfway between prince and frog.

"Jesus Christ," he said. He may or may not have been talking to me. He wasn't looking at me, but I don't think he'd have bothered looking at me if I had had a live chicken perched on my shoulder. Nothing was going to make him take his eyes off Tulip.

"Jesus," he said again, reverently. "Never saw anything like that. Longest legs I ever seen in my life.

Biggest tits I ever seen in my life. Jesus Christ on wheels."

The barmaid came over. A record ended and another began without interruption and Tulip went on doing creative things with her body. The barmaid wasn't a beast herself, a slim redhead wearing black fishnet tights and a black body stocking. She had a heart-shaped face and almond eyes, and I got the feeling that she'd spent her last incarnation as a cat. I started to think of all the different ways I could rub her to make her purr, but she was shifting her feet impatiently, and I decided that my heart (among other parts of me) already belonged to Tulip. I didn't want to spread myself too thin.

"Bottle of beer," I said.

I probably would have preferred something like whiskey and water but Tulip had warned me against it. "They make all the whiskey in New Jersey," she had said, "and it all comes out tasting like something you use to take the old finish off furniture, and then they water it, and then they serve it in shot glasses with false bottoms, and then they charge two dollars a drink for it." So I ordered beer, which came straight from the brewery in a nice hygienic bottle. It also cost two dollars a copy, which is a little high for beer, but it was a business expense if there ever was one so I didn't mind.

"Just look at that bush," my companion said. "Soft

and blond and gorgeous. I wonder is she gonna do a spread."

I was rather hoping she wasn't. I was feeling rather weird, if you want to know. On the one hand Tulip was turning me on with her dancing and all, and on the other hand I was a little upset about the fact that this was someone whom I knew personally and professionally, and whom I sort of wanted to know a lot better in the future, and here she was not only turning me on but also turning on a whole roomful of creeps, including this particular creep next to me.

"Some clubs they come right up on the bar," the creep said. He must have been about forty-five, and he had a pencil-line moustache that was really pretty offensive. I noticed he was wearing a wedding ring. "Right up on the bar," he went on, and I still didn't know if he was talking to himself or to me or to the man on the other side of him. "Right up on the bar," he said again, "and you give 'em a tip, you slip 'em a buck, and they squat down so you can eat 'em. Go right down the line and everybody who wants to slip 'em a buck and goes ahead and has theirselves a taste."

I thought seriously about hitting him. Half-seriously, anyway. I'm not particularly good at hitting people, and also he couldn't possibly know that he was talking about the girl I fully intended to be in love with.

"Love to eat this one," he said. "Start at her toes and go clear to her nose. Then go back down again."

He went on like this. He got into some rather clinical anatomical detail and I gave some further thought to hitting him. Or I could do something less extreme. I could tip my beer into his lap, for example.

It was about that time that Tulip noticed I was there. You might have thought she would have spotted me right off, but you have to remember that she was up on an elevated platform with a bright spotlight in her eyes, and that the rest of the room was dark. Also she was off to the side so that I was not standing directly in front of her. But she did notice me now, and for a second I thought she was going to blush a little, but I guess when you do this sort of thing five nights out of seven you lose the capacity to blush, because instead she just flashed me a little half-smile and tipped me a wink and went on dancing.

This time the creep did turn to me. "See that?" he said. "I'll be a son of a bitch. The cunt is crazy about me."

"Huh?"

"She winked at me," he said. "She smiled at me. Some of these broads, they wink at everybody, but that's the first since she came on and she was smiling straight at me. What do you bet she comes over here after her number's done? Man, I'm gonna get lucky tonight. I can feel it."

The thing is, I happened to know that she *would* come over after her number. This wasn't standard; one of the good things about the Treasure Chest, from the dancers' point of view, was that you didn't have to work the bar hustling drinks between numbers. A lot of the clubs worked that way but not Treasure Chest, which was one of the reasons Tulip and her roommate Cherry were willing to work there. But Tulip would come over to meet me because we had arranged it that way, and the last thing I wanted was for her to be confronted by this idiot who was convinced she was crazy about him.

I said, "It was me she smiled at."

His mouth spread in an unpleasant grin. "You? You gotta be kidding."

"She was smiling at me."

"A young punk like you? Don't make me laugh."

"She's my sister," I said.

The grin went away, reversing itself in slow motion.

"My sister," I said again, "and I don't much care for the way you were talking about her."

"Listen," he said, "don't get me wrong. A person, you know, a person'll make remarks—"

"What I was thinking," I said, "is this. I was thinking about taking my knife out of my pocket and cutting you a little. Just a little bit."

"Listen," he said. He got off his stool and edged away from the bar. "Listen," he said, "the last thing I want is trouble."

"Maybe you ought to go home," I said.

"Jesus," he said. He headed for the door but he went most of the way walking backward so that he could keep his eyes on me and make sure my hand didn't come out of my pocket. It's awkward walking like that, and he kept stumbling but not quite falling down, and at the door he turned and fled.

I let out my breath and took my hand out of my pocket. I *had* been holding a knife in it, as a matter of fact. The knife is attached to my key chain. It's an inch long, and it has a half-inch blade. It takes about a minute to get the thing open, and I usually break my fingernails in the attempt. Haig gave it to me once. I've never figured out a use for it, but you never know when something will come in handy. I doubt that it would be the greatest thing in the world for cutting someone open with. You'd be better stabbing him with one of the keys on the chain.

A few seconds later the barmaid turned up. She pointed to the creep's half-finished drink and the pile of bills next to it. There was a ten in the pile and five or six singles.

"He coming back?"

"Not without a gun."

"Pardon me?"

"He had to leave in a hurry," I said. "He remembered a previous engagement."

"He forgot his change."

"It's for you," I said.

"It is now," she said, scooping up the bills and change. "What do you know."

"No, he meant it for you," I said.

"Oh, yeah?"

"That's what he said."

"What do you know," she said. "I pegged him for El Cheapo. You never know, do you?"

"I guess not," I said.

I sipped at my beer and turned my eyes to Tulip again. Or they turned that way of their own accord, without my having much to do with it. The music was moving toward a climax, and so was half the audience. There was a little rumble of encouragement from my fellow patrons at the bar. You could make out little encouraging show biz phrases like "Show me that pretty pussy, baby," and other tasteful bons mots. Tulip had her head back, her long blond hair swaying from side to side behind her, her large breasts pointing at the ceiling in a way that would have forced Newton to reappraise the Law of Gravity. Her whole body shuddered, and the record hit its final grooves, and she put her hands on her thighs and opened herself to the band of dirty old men, and I told myself to close my eyes, and didn't, and I'm sure it was my imagination but I thought I could see all the way to her throat.

Then the lights went out.

There was quite a bit of applause. Not a roar or anything, but more than a polite ovation. A few of my fellow voyeurs scooped change from the bar and headed for the exit. Most of us stayed where we were. The lights had only stayed off for a second, and another record had already been cued and started up, more of the same monotonous rock. If that's the music of my generation, then I guess I'm a throwback or something.

There was no emcee. I had been sort of afraid of some Neanderthal in a checkered sport coat coming up and telling dirty jokes, but Treasure Chest stuck with the basics; when one girl went off, another one came on. A male voice came over the loudspeaker and said, "That was Miss Tulip Willing, ladies and gentlemen. Let's have a big hand for her now. Tulip Willing." I looked around the club for the ladies he'd been talking about and didn't see a one. I suppose there might have been some at the tables but there certainly weren't any at the bar. Nor, for that matter, did I see anybody I would be inclined to label a gentleman. The audience gave Tulip another weaker round of applause in response to his request, and as it died out he said, "And now, ladies and gentlemen, for your viewing pleasure here at the one and only Treasure Chest, a girl with a chestful of pleasure, a pint-sized lady with queen-sized attributes, the one and only Cherry Bounce."

A pair of curtains parted and Tulip's roommate stepped into the spotlight. I knew she was Tulip's roommate because Tulip had told me so. I was seeing her for the first time and my immediate reaction was to wish that she was *my* roommate.

She was a tremendous contrast to Tulip. Tulip was

about six feet tall, give or take an inch, and Cherry was maybe five-two in platform shoes. Tulip's hair was long and blond, Cherry's short and jet black. Tulip was built on a grand scale, reminding you that you can't have too much of a good thing, and Cherry was slim, pointing out that good things come in small packages. The one thing that both of them made you dramatically aware of was that human beings are mammals.

She started to dance. She was naked, incidentally. I guess I didn't mention that. I understand that some of the topless-bottomless clubs start out with the girls wearing something, but Treasure Chest kept it simple. She was naked, and she started dancing, and as grubby as the club was and as much as I disliked the music and atmosphere, I decided there were places I would be less happy to be.

The thing is, she was a pretty good dancer. Tulip had moved around nicely and all, but what she was there for was to show you her body and the dancing was more or less incidental. With Cherry, the whole performance was enhanced by the fact that she could really dance. I don't know if this made any difference to the rest of the crowd but I noticed it and I suppose in some way it heightened my reaction to her.

"That's my roommate," a voice said.

A hand touched my arm. I turned to see Tulip standing beside me. She was wearing clothes, but not the jeans and Beethoven tee-shirt I had seen her in earlier.

Now she wore a loose-fitting navy dress. You still got a fair idea of what was lurking beneath the dress, but it was a good deal less obvious.

"Oh, hi," I said.

"Hi yourself. I gather you like my roommate."

"Uh."

"She's pretty, isn't she?"

"Uh, yeah. She's, uh, pretty."

I had been wondering what it would be like when Tulip joined me at the bar. I more or less expected some aggravation from the other males, which was why I had been moved to do the number on the creep with the thin moustache. But evidently men who get off on staring at naked girls are unsettled to be in the company of those very girls, naked or otherwise, and nobody tried to sit in on our conversation. As a matter of fact, the fat man on Tulip's right actually moved a stool away.

"Cherry dances better than I do," she said.

"I thought you danced very well."

"Oh, come on, Chip. You're sweet, but I'm not a dancer. I'm just up there to wiggle my tits and ass at the customers. That's really all it is."

"Well, uh—"

"Cherry's a real dancer. Look how graceful she is." I looked. "The trouble with Cherry is she thinks this is going to lead her to a career in dance. At least I have a realistic attitude. This is an easy way to make a dollar and not much more. Cherry thinks she can make the easy dollar and still use the place as a stepping stone. But she's generally naïve, you know. I take a harder line on reality."

I didn't take any kind of line on reality at that point. What I took was a sip of beer. I did this carefully. I don't know if I'm Mr. Ultra Cool generally, but we had established earlier that whatever cool I normally possessed tended to get lost when Tulip was in the immediate vicinity. So I sipped the beer carefully to avoid gagging on it if she said something disarming.

"Did you like my act, Chip?"

"Yes. Very much."

"Did it turn you on?"

When I didn't answer she said, "I'm not asking because I'm trying to embarrass you. It's just that I'm trying to understand the particular head of the men who come here. You know, like I don't think I would get off watching a man dance around naked. I can't say for certain because I never watched that, although I was reading where a bar at one of the big midwestern colleges has one night a week with male nude dancers, and the college girls go there and really get off on the whole thing. So maybe it would get me excited, but I don't think so. In fact I don't think those college girls would get off after the first few times. Like they would be getting off on the *idea* of it, you know, but after it became a frequent thing it would be boring for them."

"I see what you mean."

"But men really get off looking at naked women, don't they?"

I glanced briefly at the absorbed men on either side of us. "Evidently," I said.

"So I wasn't asking to put you on the spot. But you seem like a sane, healthy guy, and I was wondering how you reacted, because sometimes I'm inclined to think of the general audience here as a batch of perverts, which may or may not be fair of me, and I was wondering how someone like you would react."

I didn't know exactly what to say, because I didn't know what my reaction was, exactly. It had been a turn-on watching her on stage, but then it had been at least as exciting in many ways being with her that afternoon, and it was hard to decide whether I would have reacted to her the same way on stage if she had been a total stranger instead of someone who had already Put Ideas In My Head. In some ways it might have been more of a turn-on if I hadn't known her, especially at the end when she did the spread number. That might have been a turn-off in any context—it was sort of humiliating and demeaning and like that—but how could I tell? If it was a total stranger up there I might have gone ape like all the other card-carrying sex maniacs in the audience.

I tried to judge some of this on the basis of my reaction to Cherry, but that didn't really work either. Because even though I hadn't met her she was already someone I knew by proxy. I had stood in her messy bedroom, I had pictured her in my mind, so it wasn't the same thing.

I was trying to decide how all this worked, and how much of it I wanted to mention to Tulip, when the barmaid turned up and asked if I was ready for another beer. I still had a half-filled glass and there was some left in the bottle, so what she meant was that I was drinking too slowly and the joint wasn't in business for its health.

"Chip's with me," Tulip said. "You can let up on the salesmanship number, Jan."

"Sorry about that," Jan said, and winked. "Didn't know."

I smiled back, and we sort of carried on a conversation without getting back to the subject Tulip had raised. She said that Cherry would join us after the show. It was her last number, and we could all get the hell out and go someplace quiet for coffee, and I could ask Cherry various questions and we could see if we learned anything.

"It should be fascinating," she said. "I've always wanted to see how a detective works."

"Well, you know the questions Haig and I asked you this afternoon."

"Oh, this is different. I mean, I was the one you were asking questions. I'll be watching you ask questions of somebody else and that should make a big difference."

"Maybe."

"Do you know what questions you're going to ask

her?" I was looking for an answer to that one when Cherry's first number ended. There was a round of applause approximately equal in volume to what Tulip got, and then another record was cued and Cherry went into her second and last number.

"Do you know what questions you're going to ask her, Chip?"

I knew what questions I wanted to ask her. I wanted to ask her where she'd been all my life. She was putting a little more sex into her routine on this number, letting her hands glide upward from the sides of her thighs to her genuinely impressive breasts, and giving little ooohs and ahhhs to indicate that she was turning herself on. I don't know if she was really turning herself on, but I can swear to you that she was turning me on, and I don't think I was the only person in the audience who was having that reaction.

"Chip?"

"Er," I said. "Uh, with questions and all that. You sort of have to play it by ear."

"I see."

"It's best not to have everything all scheduled in advance like a presidential press conference or something. You sort of see how one question leads to another."

"It sounds fascinating."

I was glad she thought it was fascinating, because what I thought it was was bullshit. The fact of the matter was that I didn't have the foggiest idea what I was going to ask Cherry, or even why. The more I thought about this case of ours, the more I found myself leaning toward the conclusion that Leo Haig had finally done it. He'd finally slipped over that thin line between genius and insanity, because we never should have taken this absurd case in the first place, because—no matter who Tulip Willing happened to be in her spare time—there was absolutely no excuse for investigating a case involving—

"Chip?"

I broke off my reverie and looked at her. "What?"

"Is Cherry a suspect?"

"Everybody's a suspect."

"Because it's hard to believe she could commit murder."

I looked at her, and I decided it wasn't at all hard to believe that she could commit murder. Not directly, but I could see where she could hand out coronaries to half her audience every night just by doing what she was doing.

I said, "There's one thing you have to realize. Everybody's a suspect until proven otherwise."

"I thought everyone's innocent until proved guilty."

"Absolutely. And everybody's suspicious until proved innocent. That's how it works. Cherry's a suspect, Glenn Flatt's a suspect. Haskell Henderson's a suspect. So's his wife. That Danzig is a suspect. Simon What's-his-name—"

"Barckover."

"Barckover, right." I was supposed to remember things like Barckover's last name, Haig had told me, just as I was supposed to be able to repeat all conversations verbatim. If Archie Goodwin can do something, I'm supposed to train myself to do it, too. (Sometimes, let me tell you, Archie Goodwin gives me a stiff pain.) "Barckover," I said again, carefully training my memory. "And Andrew Merganser—"

"You mean Mallard."

"Well, I knew it was some kind of a duck. The hell with Archie Goodwin."

"Pardon me?"

"Forget it," I said, a little more savagely than I'd intended. "Mallard and Helen Tattersall and Gus Leemy and whoever the hell else you mentioned. Everybody—"

"Don't say Gus's name so loud. He's probably in the club tonight."

"Well, they're all suspects," I said, not so loud this time around. "And so are other people we haven't even thought of yet, and one of them's a killer."

"It's still hard to believe."

I let the conversation die there. If she thought that was hard to believe, she didn't know the half of it. What I found hard to believe was that Haig and I were involved. True, Haig was only really happy when he had a murder case to bother his brain with. And true, this case involved murder, and not just one murder, not just another murder, but—

Tulip's fingers closed on my elbow. "Watch now, Chip. She's coming to the end and she really makes a production out of it. She shows a lot more than I do. Watch!"

So I watched. I mean, maybe you would have looked up at the ceiling or something. Anything's possible. But what I did, see, is I watched.

Watched as she lowered herself first to her knees, then lay almost full-length, her perfect breasts suspended over the apron of the stage. Watched her straighten up and swing that body around, shaking those breasts from side to side, always perfectly in time to that awful music. Watched as she displayed herself, giving everybody a much longer look than everybody needed. Watched as she put one little hand to her mouth, miming shock at what she had done, straightening up now, drawing herself primly together, her shoulders held back to bring her breasts into the sharpest possible relief.

And heard her sudden gasp.

And saw the bead of blood on her left breast just an inch above the nipple. And watched her hands, moving in awful slow motion, struggling to touch the bead of blood.

And watched her fall, still in slow motion, falling backwards and to her left, falling as only dead things fall, landing at last on the floorboards of the stage with the impact of a gunshot.

* * *

I guess my reaction time was pretty good. It didn't seem to be at the time, but the fact remains that I was the first person to vault the bar and leap onto the stage and have a look at Cherry Bounce.

On the other hand, fast or slow, my reaction was wrong. What I should have done was forget the stage entirely and go straight to the door to keep anybody else from going through it. Because I had seen the way Cherry tried to reach her breast and couldn't, and I had seen her fall, and I really didn't have to go up onto the stage to examine her in order to know there was nothing I could do for her.

Haig has always said it's nothing to berate myself for. He says anybody's natural and proper reaction is to establish first of all that the victim is beyond assistance. Well, that was my reaction, all right, and that was what I established.

Our murderer had just claimed his one hundred twenty-fourth victim, and he had done it right in front of my eyes.

Two

WHEN THE DOORBELL rang that afternoon I was spooning brine shrimp into a tank of *Labeo chrysophekadion*. They were cute little rascals, about half an inch long, and most people who keep tropical fish call them black sharks. Which is sort of weird, because they are not sharks at all and in no sense sharklike, being peaceful types who function as scavengers in an aquarium, picking up on food that other fish have missed. Ours weren't black, either, but white and pink-eyed like Easter bunnies. Leo Haig had come up with a couple of albinos in an earlier spawning, and now he had bred them to each other, and the two hundred or so fish I was presently feeding were the result.

Haig couldn't have been prouder if he had sired them himself. I was kind of pleased with them too, but I couldn't see what they had to do with Being a Resourceful Private Detective, which was what I was supposed to be. When I would bring up the subject Haig would tell me that the aquarium was the universe in microcosm, and the lessons it taught me would ultimately find application in life itself. He says things like that a lot.

Anyway, the doorbell rang. I gave the unblack unsharks a last spoonful of brine shrimp and went to the door and opened it, and it was good I had left the spoon and the saucer of shrimp in the other room, because otherwise I would have dropped them.

Instead I dropped my jaw. I stood there with my mouth open and stared at her.

There was a whole lot of her to stare at. I'm reasonably tall, although no one would mistake me for a professional basketball player, and she was just about my height. There the resemblance ended. She had long golden hair framing a face with absolutely nothing wrong with it. High cheekbones, wide-set blue eyes the color of a New York sky at sunset, a complexion out of an advertisement for sun-tan lotion, a mouth out of an advertisement for fellatio.

The part below the face was no disappointment, either. She was wearing jeans and a Beethoven-for-President tee-shirt, and she wasn't wearing anything under the tee-shirt, and I really couldn't find anything about her body to object to. I suppose a purist might argue that her legs were a little too long and her breasts were a little too large. Somehow this didn't bother me a bit.

For a while she watched me stare at her. She gave a

sort of half-smile, which suggested that she was used to this reaction but liked it all the same, and then she said, "Mr. Haig?"

"No."

"Pardon me?"

"I'm not him. I mean, I'm me. Uh."

"Perhaps I came at a bad time."

"Oh, no," I said. "You came at a wonderful time. I mean you can come anytime you want to. I mean. Uh."

"Is this Leo Haig's residence?"

"Yes."

"Leo Haig the detective?"

He's Leo Haig the detective all right, but that's not a phrase that rolls off most people's tongues. As a matter of fact he's pretty close to being an unknown, which is not the way he wants it, and one of the main reasons he hired me as his assistant. A chief function of mine is to write up his cases—at least the ones that turn out triumphant—so that the world will know about him. If it weren't for Dr. Watson, he says, who would have heard of Sherlock Holmes? If Archie Goodwin never sat down at a typewriter, who would be aware of Nero Wolfe? Anyway, that's why he hired me, to make Leo Haig The Detective a household phrase, and that's how come you get to read all this.

"Leo Haig the detective," I agreed.

"Then I came to the right place," she said.

"Oh, definitely. No question about it. You came to the right place."

"Are you all right?"

"Oh, sure. I'm terrific."

"May I come in?"

"Oh, sure. Right. Great idea."

She gave me an odd look, which I certainly deserved, and I stood aside and she came in and I closed the door. I led her into the office which Haig and I share. There's a huge old partner's desk, which we also share, although I don't really have much use for my side of it. I pointed to a chair for her, and when she sat down I swiveled my desk chair around and sat in it and looked at her some more. She was a little less intimidating when she was sitting down. There was still just as much of her but the overall effect was not quite so awesome.

"Is Mr. Haig in?"

"He's upstairs," I said. "He's playing with his fish."

"Playing with them?"

"Sort of. I'm his assistant. My name is Harrison. Chip Harrison."

"Mine is Tulip."

"Oh."

"Tulip Willing."

"It certainly is," I said.

"Pardon me?"

I was really having a difficult time getting my brain

in gear. I took a deep breath and tried again. I said, "You wanted to see Mr. Haig?"

"That's right. I want to hire him."

"I see."

"There's a matter that I want him to investigate."

"I see," I said again. "Could you tell me something about the matter?"

"Well—"

"I'm his assistant," I said. "His confidential assistant."

"Aren't you young to be a detective?"

I'm not exactly a detective. I mean I don't have a license or anything. But I didn't see any point in telling her that. What I wanted to say was that you don't have to be all that old to spoon brine shrimp into a fish tank, but I didn't say that either. I said, "If you could give me some idea—"

"Of course." She leaned forward and I took another quick look at Beethoven's eyebrows. Her breasts had fantastic stage presence. It was hard not to stare at them, and you sort of got the feeling they were staring back.

"It's a murder case," she said.

I don't know if my heartbeat actually quickened, because it had been operating faster than normal ever since I opened the door and took my first look at her. But I certainly did get excited. I mean, people don't generally turn up on our doorstep wanting us to investigate a murder. But it happens all the time in books, and that's the kind of detective Haig wants to be, the kind you read about in mystery novels.

I said, "A homicide."

"Not exactly."

"I thought you said a murder."

She nodded. "But homicide means that a person has been killed, doesn't it?"

"I think so."

"Well, this is murder. But it's not homicide."

"I don't think I understand."

She put her hand to her mouth and nibbled thoughtfully at a cuticle. If she ever ran out of cuticles to nibble I decided I'd gladly lend her one of mine. Or any other part of me that interested her. "It's hard to say this," she said.

I waited her out.

"I had to come to Leo Haig," she said eventually. "I couldn't go to the police. I never even considered going to the police. Even if they didn't actually laugh at me there's no way they would bother investigating. So I had to go to a private detective, and I couldn't go to an ordinary private detective. It has to be Leo Haig."

That's the kind of thing you want every client to say, but Tulip Willing was the first one ever to say it.

"I guess the only way to say it is to come right out with it," she said. "Someone murdered my tropical fish. I want Leo Haig to catch the killer."

* * *

I climbed a flight of stairs to the fourth floor, where Haig was playing with his fish. There are tanks in all the rooms on the third floor, but on the fourth floor there are nothing but tanks, rows and rows of them. I found Haig glowering at a school of cichlids from Lake Tanganyika. They had set him back about fifty bucks a fish, which is a lot, and no one had yet induced them to spawn in captivity. Haig intended to be the first, and thus far the fish had shown no sign of preparing to cooperate.

"There's an element missing," he said. "Maybe the rockwork should be extended. Maybe they're accustomed to spawning in caves. Maybe they want less light."

"Maybe they're all boys," I suggested.

"Phooey. There are eight of them. With six fish one is mathematically certain of having a pair. That is to say that the certainty is in excess of ninety-five percent. With eight the certainty is that much greater."

"Unless the cunning Africans only ship one sex."

He looked at me. "You have a devious mind," he said. "It will be an asset professionally."

"I have a devious mind," I agreed. "You have a client."

"Oh?"

"A beautiful young woman," I said.

"Trust you to notice that."

"I wouldn't trust anyone who didn't notice. Her name is Tulip Willing."

"Indeed."

"She wants you to investigate a murder and trap a killer."

He bounced to his feet, and the African cichlids no longer meant a thing to him. He's about five feet tall and built like a beachball, with a neatly trimmed little black goatee and head of wiry black hair. He likes to touch the beard, and he started doing it now.

"A homicide," he said.

I didn't make the distinction between murder and homicide. "She says only Leo Haig can help her," I went on. "She hasn't been to the police. She needs a private detective, and you're the only man on earth who can possibly do the job for her."

"She honestly said that?"

"Her very words."

"Remarkable."

"She's in the office. I told her I was sure you would want to talk to her yourself."

"Of course I want to talk to her." He was on his way to the stairs and even though his legs are about half the length of mine I had to hustle to catch up with him.

"One thing you ought to know before you talk to her," I said.

"Oh?"

"About the victims."

He was positively beaming. "Victims? Plural? More than one victim?"

"Over a hundred of them."

He stared, and his face showed a struggle between delight and disbelief. He really wanted it to be a murder case with a hundred victims, and at the same time he was beginning to read the whole number as a put-on.

"One thing you ought to know," I said. "The victims aren't people. They're fish."

He said, "Miss Willing? I'm Leo Haig. I believe you've already met my assistant, Mr. Harrison."

"Yes, I have."

"I understand some fishes of yours were murdered. Could you give me some specific information on the crime?"

I had to hand it to him. I don't know what kind of reaction I'd been hoping for but it wasn't what I got. I had sent him up in a pretty rotten way, when you stop to think of it, and he was returning the favor by treating Tulip Willing and her massacred fish like the crime of the century. Instead of telling me to get rid of her, either by showing her the door or calling the men in the white coats, he was going to take his time getting her whole story, and I was going to have to write it all down in my notebook. I made it game, set and match to him.

So I sat there with my notebook on my side of the desk, and Haig sat on his side of the desk and played with a pipe, and Tulip Willing sat in the chair I'd put her in originally. I sensed that the three of us were

going to waste an hour or so of each other's time. I
didn't really mind. I hadn't been doing anything that
sensational with my time in the first place, and I
couldn't think of anyone I'd rather waste it with.
(Than Tulip, I mean. Wasting time with Haig is something I do almost every day of my life. It's enjoyable,
but there's nothing all that exotic about it.)

"There are many ways an entire tank of fishes can be
destroyed at once," he was saying. He has this profes-
sorial air that he likes to use. "Certain diseases strike
with the rapidity and force of the Black Death, wiping
out a whole fish population overnight. Air pollution,
paint fumes, these can cause annihilation on an extraordinary scale."

"Mr. Haig—"

"Occasionally equipment malfunctions. A thermo-
stat may go haywire, boiling the inhabitants of an
aquarium. On the other hand, a heater may burn out
and the resulting drop in temperature may prove fatal,
although this is more likely to be a gradual matter. In
other situations—"

"Mr. Haig, I'm not an idiot."

"I didn't mean to imply that you were."

"I'm familiar with the ways fishes can die. Naturally
you would assume that the death was accidental. I
made the same assumption myself. I ruled out the
possibilities of natural and accidental death."

"Indeed."

"The fish were poisoned."

He took his pipe apart. He's given up smoking them because they burn his tongue, but he likes to fiddle with them. He bought the pipes originally because he thought they might be a good character tag and he knows that great detectives have to have charming idiosyncracies. He keeps trying on idiosyncracies looking for one that will fit. I've wanted to tell him that he's odd enough all by himself, but I can't think of an acceptable way to phrase it.

I waited for him to ask how she knew the fish were poisoned. Instead he said, "What sort of fish? A community tank, I suppose? Mollies and swordtails and the like?"

"No. I don't have a community tank. These were Scats."

"Ah. *Scatophagus argus.*"

"These were *Scatophagus tetracanthus*, actually."

"Indeed." He seemed impressed. He thinks everybody should know the Latin name of everything, and I get a lecture to that effect on the average of once every three days. "The *tetracanthus* are imported less often. And most retailers sell them as *argus* because few hobbyists know the difference. These were definitely *tetracanthus*, you say?"

"Yes."

"How many did you have?"

"One hundred twenty-three."

"Indeed. You must be rather fond of the species. You must also have had an extremely large tank."

"It's a twenty-nine gallon tank."

He frowned. "Good heavens," he said. "You must have stacked them like cordwood."

"All but two were fry. They had plenty of room."

"Fry?" His eyebrows went up, first at the word she used, then at the implications. Most people who keep fish, and certainly most people who look anything like Tulip Willing, call baby fish baby fish. She called them fry. Then, when the whole idea sank in, he leaned forward and waggled a finger at her. "Impossible," he said.

"What's impossible?"

"Neither of the *Scatophagus* species has ever spawned in captivity."

"I spawned them. And it's been done before."

"By Rachow, yes. But he had an accident and lost the lot, and he was never able to repeat the procedure. Nor has anyone else had any success."

"I had success," she said.

"Impossible," he said again. "No one but Rachow ever induced the little devils to spawn. And he was working with *argus*, not *tetracanthus*." He paused abruptly and his eyes crawled upward and examined the ceiling. "Wait just one moment," he said. "Just one moment."

I looked at Tulip and watched her wait one moment. There was the hint of a private smile on her lips.

"There *was* a spawning," he said finally. "Not of *ar-*

gus. Of *tetracanthus*. It was reported in *Copeia* a year ago. The fish spawned but a fungus destroyed the spawn before they hatched. The author was—let me think. Wolinski. T. J. Wolinski. He's done other articles for aquarist publications."

"Not he," Tulip said.

"Pardon me?"

She was really smiling now. "Not *he*," she repeated. "She. Me, actually. They spawned a second time and I used a fungicide and it worked. I got a seventy percent hatch. One hundred twenty-one fry, and they were doing beautifully. I left the parent fish with them."

"Your name is Willing. Tulip Willing."

"That's a stage name."

"And your real name is—"

"Thelma Wolinski."

Haig was on his feet, his jaw set firmly beneath the neat little beard. "T. J. Wolinski," he said, with something verging on reverence. "T. J. Wolinski. Extraordinary. And some creature poisoned your scats? Good heavens. You'll pardon me, I hope, for treating you like a witling. I never would have guessed—well, that's by the way. Some villain poisoned your fishes, did he? Well, we shall get to the bottom of this. And I shall have his head, madam. Rest assured of that. I shall have his head."

So the whole thing was out of control. It was my fault, and although there was a certain amount of thrill in the idea of being on a case, I can't say I was anywhere near as thrilled as Haig was.

Well, I'd asked for it. I'd been baiting him, never figuring he'd bite, and now he was hooked right through the gills.

Three

IT MUST HAVE been around three in the afternoon when Tulip Willing rang the doorbell. It was close to five when Haig was finished asking questions. He went over everything and enabled me to fill a great many pages in my notebook with facts that would probably turn out to be unimportant. It's his theory that there is no such thing as an absolutely inconsequential fact. (The first time he told me this I replied that in 1938 the state of Wyoming produced one-third of a pound of dry edible beans for every man, woman, and child in the nation. He agreed that it was certainly hard to see how that could turn out to be consequential, but he wasn't going to rule out the possibility entirely.)

I'm taking matters into my own hands and leaving out some items that never did seem to have any more bearing on the case than the fascinating fact about dry edible beans. That still leaves plenty of bits and pieces to report from Haig's questioning of Tulip.

Item: The fish had died four days ago, on a Saturday. Tulip had come home at four Saturday morning after a long night at the Treasure Chest, where she had been working for five months, having been previously employed in a similar capacity at similar nightspots, among them Tippler's Cove and Shake It Or Leave It. (I am not making any of this up.) She came home, exhausted and ready for bed, and she went over to say goodnight to the fish, and they were all floating on the top, which is never a sign of radiant good health. When she was done being hysterical she did something intelligent. She removed the two parent fish and preserved them in jars of rubbing alcohol in case an autopsy should ultimately be indicated, and she took a sample of the water in the tank and another sample of water from another aquarium as a control. These she took to a chemical laboratory on Varick Street for scientific analysis, and Monday the laboratory called her and informed her that the sample from the tank of scats contained strychnine, which is no better for fish than it is for people. There was enough strychnine present to kill any human being who drank a glass of the water, but then not that many people go around drinking out of aquariums, and I'd venture to say that those who do are asking for it.

Item: She assumed that the murder of the scats was motivated not by a specific hatred of the fish themselves but by hatred of their owner. Someone was trying to upset her or punish her or terrify her by killing her pets. This was, as far as she could determine, the first instance of hostile behavior to be directed at her, aside from the usual obscene telephone calls she received intermittently. The phone calls had not increased in frequency lately, and in fact she hadn't heard from one of the callers in a long time and was a little concerned that something might have happened to him. She said that he had a very unusual approach, but she didn't go into detail.

Item: The scats had been in fine fettle when she left the apartment Friday afternoon at two o'clock. The strychnine would presumably have worked instantly upon its introduction into the aquarium, but she had been unable to determine just how long the fish had been dead. So somewhere between two Friday afternoon and four Saturday morning the villain had entered her apartment and had done the dirty deed.

Item: While I don't guess there was anybody who could properly be labeled a suspect at this stage of the game, the following people were sufficiently a part of Tulip's life to find their way into my notebook:

Cherry Bounce. I know, I know, but if you can accept a name like Tulip Willing, why be put off by Cherry Bounce? Cherry and Tulip had been roommates for just about five months. They met when Tulip went to work at Treasure Chest, where Cherry had already been employed. Tulip had recently broken up with her boyfriend and needed a place to live, and Cherry had recently broken up with a boyfriend of her own and needed someone to share her rent. The two of them had been getting along well enough, although they didn't have much in common outside of their profession. Tulip characterized her as flighty, flitting from one pursuit to another, health foods to astrology to bio-feedback. As far as the fish were concerned, Cherry thought they were cute. Cherry's name off-stage was Mabel Abramowicz, so I guess she would have had to change it to something.

Glenn Flatt. Tulip's ex-husband, whom she had met and married four years ago when she was picking up a doctorate in marine biology at the University of Miami, and whom she had divorced two years later. I could understand why she had divorced him—she wanted her own name back. No one built like Tulip could be happy with Flatt for a surname. (According to her, she left her husband because he was a compulsive gambler. If you said *Good Morning* to him he'd lay odds that it wasn't. This would have been all right if he won, but he evidently didn't.) Flatt lived on Long Island where he was employed as a research biochemist by a pharmaceutical manufacturer. This fact prompted Haig and me to glance meaningfully at each other—Flatt's job would undoubtedly give him access to strychnine. On the other hand, it would probably give him just as good access to any number of nondetectable vehicles for ichthyicide. Flatt and Tulip were "very good friends now," she said, and they occasionally had dinner or drinks together, and now and then he turned up at the club to catch her act. Flatt had never remarried.

Haskell Henderson. Tulip's current boyfriend and the owner of a half-dozen local health food stores. They had been seeing each other for almost three months. Henderson would spend two or three afternoons a week at Tulip's apartment. I don't guess he devoted much of this time to staring at the fish. When he wasn't keeping company with Tulip or minding the stores he was in Closter, New Jersey, where he shared a cozy little house with . . .

Mrs. Haskell Henderson. Tulip had never met Mrs. H.H., and had no way of knowing whether or not the woman even knew of her existence, but anyone with that sound a reason for wanting unpleasant things to happen to Tulip certainly deserved an entry in my notebook. The entry was pretty much limited to her name because Henderson evidently didn't talk about his wife very much.

Simon Barckover. Tulip's agent, and Cherry's agent too, for that matter. His relationship with both clients was strictly professional, but he got in the notebook because he was the only person around who might have a specific grudge against the fish. He thought Tulip was genuinely talented and that she had a future in show business if she applied herself. Tulip admitted that he might be right but she wasn't interested. The

topless dancing paid well and was generally undemanding, leaving her free to concentrate on her chief
interest, which was ichthyology. Barckover had told
her on several occasions that the damn fish were standing in the way of her career and that he would like to
flush the lot of them down the toilet. She couldn't believe he would actually do it, but then she couldn't
believe anybody would want to poison the scats, so he
got in the notebook.

Leonard Danzig. Cherry's boyfriend. She had been
dating him for a month or so, although she continued
to see other men as well. He got on the list because
Tulip couldn't stand him, describing him charitably as
"a kind of a slimy character." I gather she disliked him
because he kept trying to get her into bed, either just
with him or with Cherry along for threesies. Tulip was
spectacularly uninterested in either prospect. No one
seemed to know what Danzig did for a living, but
Tulip guessed it was at least somewhat criminal.
Cherry had met him at the club. He always seemed to
have a lot of money, and if he worked at all he didn't
seem to have any set hours. His feelings toward the
fish were unknown, except that he had once remarked
that it would "take a hell of a lot of the bastards to
make a decent meal."

Helen Tattersall. All that Tulip knew about Mrs. Tattersall was that she lived in the apartment immediately below hers and was a pain in the ass, constantly

complaining about noise, even when no noise whatsoever was emanating from the apartment. She had on one occasion reported Tulip and Cherry to the police, alleging that the two were running a bordello in their apartment. Tulip wasn't sure whether the woman actually believed this or was just making a nuisance of herself. "She's the sort of frustrated old bitch who might poison somebody's pets just out of meanness," Tulip said.

Andrew Mallard. Tulip's former boyfriend, the one she was living with before she got together with Cherry. He was an advertising account executive, recently divorced, and evidently rather strange. He had moved in with Tulip; then, when they broke up, she had moved out and let him keep the apartment because the idea of actually going out and finding a place of his own gave him anxiety attacks. He still called her occasionally when he was drunk, generally at an hour when he should have known she was sleeping. Now and then he caught her act at Treasure Chest, always tipping heavily in order to get a ringside table, always attending by himself, always staring at her breasts as if hypnotized, and never speaking a word to her. Every once in a while she got flowers delivered backstage with no note enclosed—though never on nights when he was in the audience—and she sort of assumed he was the source. He had liked the fish very much while they lived together, but she figured he was a possible suspect because murdering fish was clearly an insane act, and Andrew Mallard was hardly playing with a full deck himself.

Gus Leemy. He owned the Treasure Chest. At least he was the owner of record, but Tulip had the impression that the club was a Mafia joint of one sort or another and that Leemy was fronting for the real owners. She wasn't even sure he knew she had fish and couldn't imagine why he would have anything against her or them. I think she brought his name up because she didn't like him.

So I had those nine names in my notebook, and there was a fourteen-hour period of time during which any of them could have gone to Tulip's apartment and done something fishy to her fish. Possibly any or all of them could account for their time, but Tulip didn't know about it. And possibly one of the fourteen million other residents of the New York metropolitan area was the killer. I mean, if you're going to do something as fundamentally insane as feeding strychnine to tropical fish, they wouldn't have to be the fish of someone you know, would they? If you're going to be a lunatic about it, one fish tank is as good as another.

A little before five Haig leaned back in his chair and put his feet on top of his desk. I've tried to break him of this habit but it's impossible. Tulip and I sat there respectfully and studied the soles of his shoes while the great man searched for meaning in the ceiling.

Without opening his eyes he said, "Chip."

"Sir."

"I need your eyes and ears and legs. The scene of the crime must be examined. You will go with Miss Wolinski to her apartment. Miss Wolinski? I assume that will be convenient?"

Tulip agreed that it would be. She had a dinner date at eight-thirty and a performance at ten o'clock but she was free until then.

"Satisfactory," Haig said. He swung his feet down from the desk. "You will visit Miss Wolinski's apartment. You will be guided by your intelligence and intuition and experience. You will then return here to report."

"If that's all—" Tulip said.

Haig had turned to look at the Rasboras. They're little pinkish fish with dark triangles on their sides, and Haig has a ten-gallon tank of them directly behind his desk chair at eye level. He's apt to turn around and study them in the middle of a conversation. This time, though, his attention to the Rasboras was a sign that the conversation was over.

The hell it was. I said, "I'll make out a receipt for Miss Wolinski for her retainer."

Haig said, "Retainer?"

Tulip said, "Oh, of course. You'll be wanting a retainer, won't you?"

I don't know what he'd do without me. I swear I don't. The trouble is, Haig keeps forgetting that if you're going to be a detective for a living you ought to do your best to make a living out of it. For most of his life he lived in two ratty rooms in the Bronx, breeding tropical fish and trucking plastic bags around to pet shops, peddling his little babies for a nickel here and a dime there. All the while he read every mystery and detective story ever published, and then his uncle died and left him a fortune, and he bought this house and let Madam Juana keep the lower two floors and set up shop as a detective, which is terrific, no question about it. But his capital isn't really enough to keep us together, so when we get a case it's a good idea for us to get money out of it, and here he was going to let Tulip hire us without paying anything.

"Of course," Tulip said again, digging in her bag for a checkbook. When she came up with it I uncapped a pen and handed it to her. She started to make out the check, then looked up to ask the amount.

"Five hundred is standard," I said.

Haig almost fainted. I think he would have asked her for fifty bucks and let her talk him down. But the five hundred didn't phase our client for a second. I guess all she had to be told was that it was standard. She finished making out the check and passed it to me, and I wrote out a receipt on a sheet from my notebook and gave it to Haig for him to sign. He wrote his name with a flourish, as usual. Imagine what he could do if he had more than seven letters to work with.

"I intend to earn this," he said, holding the check in his pudgy little hand. "You'll receive full value for your money, Miss Wolinski. In a sense, you might say your troubles are over."

And ours are just beginning, I thought. But then Tulip got to her feet, sort of uncoiling from her chair like a trained cobra responding to a flute, and I decided that any case that forced me to go to her apartment with her couldn't possibly be all bad.

"He's quite a man," Tulip said. "It must be very inspiring to work for someone like Leo Haig."

"It's all of that," I agreed. "And do I call you Miss Wolinski or Miss Willing?"

"Call me Tulip. And may I call you Chip?"

Call me darling, I thought. "Sure," I said. "Call me Chip."

"What's that a nickname for?"

"It's the only name I've got," I said, which is certainly true now. I had started life as Leigh Harvey Harrison, both Leigh and Harvey being proper names in my less-than-proper family, but in the fall of '63 my parents decided that wouldn't do at all, and I've been Chip ever since. I understand there are a lot of Jews named Arthur who were known to the world as Adolph until sometime in the '30s.

We talked a little more about Haig, and then the cab dropped us at her building, a high-rise on the corner of 54th and Eighth. The lobby reminded you a little of an airline terminal. "It's not exactly overflowing with warmth and charm," Tulip said. "It's sort of sterile, isn't it? Before I moved here I lived in a brownstone in the Village. I really liked that apartment and I would have kept it except it would have meant keeping Andrew, too. This place has all the character of an office building, but on the other hand the elevators are fast and there's plenty of closet space and there aren't any cockroaches. My other place was crawling with them, and of course I couldn't spray because of the fish."

"Couldn't you try trapping them and feeding them to the fish?"

"Is that what Leo Haig does?"

"No, it just occurred to me. What we do, Wong Fat puts some kind of crystals in the corners of the kitchen, and the roaches eat it and die. They come from miles around to do themselves in. I don't know what Wong does with them. I suppose he throws them out." I thought for a moment. "I *hope* he throws them out."

On the elevator she told me another bad feature of the building. "There are prostitutes living here," she said. "I wouldn't mind if they just lived here. They also work here, and you can't imagine what that's like."

I could imagine.

"There are these men coming and going all the time," she said, which was probably true in more ways than she meant. "And they see a girl in the building, any girl, and they take it for granted that you're in the business yourself. It's very unpleasant."

"I'm sure it is."

"As if I didn't get enough of that aggravation at the club. Just because a girl displays her body men tend to assume that it's for sale. I mean, I don't kid myself, Chip. Cherry thinks she's an artist, she takes singing lessons and dancing lessons, the whole bit. She's waiting to be discovered. I think she's a little bit whacky. Men don't come to watch me because I'm such a sensational dancer. I'm a pretty rotten dancer, as a matter of fact. They come to see me and they pay two dollars a drink for watered rotgut because they enjoy looking at my tits."

"Oh."

"That's all it is, really. Tits."

"Uh."

"If it weren't for my tits," she said, "I'd be teaching high school biology."

I couldn't think of anything to say to that one, but as it turned out I didn't have to because we had reached her door and she was fishing in her purse for the key. She got it out, then rang the bell. "In case Cherry's home," she explained. We stood around for a while, long enough for her to conclude that Cherry wasn't home, and then she opened the door and walked inside. I didn't follow her, and she asked me what I was waiting out in the hall for.

"Just a minute," I said. I dropped to one knee and examined the lock. There were two cylinders but one was just a blind to confuse burglars. The other was a Rabson, a good one, and I couldn't find any scratches on the cylinder or on the bolt. That didn't necessarily mean the killer had had a key; if he had a good set of picks and knew how to use them he could open the lock without leaving evidence behind. "Of the nine people you mentioned before," I said, "how many have keys?"

"Oh. He got in with a key?"

"It's possible."

"So you want to know who has keys?"

I got out my notebook and went through the nine of them. Cherry had a key, of course, it being her apartment. Glenn Flatt, the ex-husband, had been to the apartment a few times but had never been given a key. Haskell Henderson, the current boyfriend, had a key. Mrs. Haskell Henderson hadn't been given one, but she could have swiped or duplicated her husband's, assuming she knew anything about it. Leonard Danzig had a key, as did any number of past and present boyfriends of Cherry's. Helen Tattersall, the neighbor, didn't, but there was always the possibility that she had access to the building's master key. There was a chainbolt on the inside of the door, but when nobody was home it wasn't locked and the master key would open the other lock.

Andrew Mallard did not have a key and had never been to the apartment. Maybe Tulip was afraid that if she ever let him in she would have to move again. Simon Barckover might well have a key, since Cherry gave them out rather indiscriminately, but Tulip wasn't

sure one way or the other. And Gus Leemy probably
didn't have a key.

"But anybody *could* have one easily enough," Tulip
said. "The thing about Cherry, she tends to misplace
things. Especially keys. I think she's borrowed my key
four times in the past five months to have duplicates
made, and she always has several made at a time.
Anyone could have borrowed her key to have a dupli-
cate made, and if he didn't put it back when he was
done she would just assume she lost it again. It's sort
of a nuisance."

"It must be."

"And then sometimes she sets the latch and doesn't
bother taking a key, and it's even possible that she
came back here Friday night to change or something
and left the door unlocked, and then came back again
and locked it. So anybody at all could have walked in.
Just some ordinary prowler, trying doors and finding
this one unlocked."

"Just some ordinary prowler looking to find an
open apartment with a fish tank he could pour strychnine into?"

"Oh."

"I think we can rule out the Ordinary Prowler
theory."

"I guess you're right. I'm not thinking very clearly."
She dropped into a chair, then bounced back up again.
And *bounced* is precisely the word to fit the act. She
bounced, and her breasts bounced, and I'd just about

reached the point where I was able to look at her without being very close to drooling, and that little bounce she did put me right back at square one again.

"I'm a terrible hostess," she said. "I didn't offer you a drink. You'll have a drink, won't you?"

"If you're having one."

"I am, but what does that have to do with it? What would you like?"

I tried not to look at the front of her tee-shirt. "I'll have a glass of milk," I said.

"Gee, I don't think we've got any."

"That's all right," I said. "I don't even like milk."

"Then why did you ask for it?"

"I don't know," I said. "The words just came out that way. I'll have whatever you're having."

"Great. I'm having bourbon and yogurt. Do you want yours on the rocks or straight up?"

"I guess on the rocks. What's so funny?"

But she didn't answer. She was too busy laughing. Most women tend to giggle, which can be pleasant enough, but Tulip put her head back and gave out with a full-scale belly laugh, and it really sounded great. While she stood there laughing her head off I rewound some mental recording tape and played back the conversation, and I said, "Oh."

"Bourbon and yogurt!"

"Very funny," I said.

"On the *rocks*!"

She actually slapped her thigh. You hear about people

doing that but I didn't think anybody really did. She laughed her head off and slapped her thigh.

"I guess I got distracted," I said.

"A glass of *milk*!"

"Look, Miss Wolinski—"

"Oh, Chip, I'm sorry." She came to me and put her hand on my arm. I didn't want to react because I wasn't feeling sexy, I was feeling mad, but what I wanted didn't have very much to do with it. She put her hand on my arm, and it was as if I'd stuck my big toe into an electrical outlet.

"I was just teasing you a little," she said.

"I hope you never tease me a lot. I don't think I could handle it."

"How about a beer?"

"Great."

I told her I'd like to look around the apartment while she poured the beer. She said that was fine. There was the living room, fairly good sized, and there were two small bedrooms, each furnished with a platform bed and a night table and a chest of drawers. The first bedroom I entered looked like an ad for disaster insurance. The bed was unmade, assuming it had ever been made to begin with, and there was so much underwear scattered around that it was hard to find the floor. I sort of hoped that was Cherry's bedroom because I didn't want to learn that our client was that much of a slob. When I looked in the other bedroom I established that it was Tulip's. It was immaculate, and there was a fish tank in it.

I sat on the edge of the bed and looked in the tank. There was a glass divider in the middle and an African Gourami on each side of it.

"Here's your beer," she said from the doorway. "Hey, did anything happen to those guys?"

There was real alarm in her voice. "They're fine," I said. "What species are they? I mean I know they're *Ctenapoma* but I don't recognize the species."

"*Ctenapoma fasciolatum.* I don't suppose he's started building a bubble nest, has he?" She came over and looked over my shoulder. "He hasn't, darn it. That's the third female I've had in there with him. He killed the other two. I used the divider when I put the second female in, and I waited until he had a nest built, and I figured that was a clear signal that he was madly and passionately in love, so I lifted out the divider and the little bastard charged right at her and killed her." She sat down on the bed next to me and gave me a glass of beer. I took a long drink of it. "So I don't really know what to do," she went on. "This time he's not even building a nest. He just ignores the poor old girl completely. And you can see she's ready to spawn. She's positively bursting with eggs, the little angel. I must be doing something wrong."

"Mr. Haig might be able to tell you."

"Has he bred *fasciolatum*?"

"No, but he's had results with some of the other *Ctenapoma* species. He has some secrets."

"Do you think he'd tell me?"

"If you told him how you managed the scats."

She grinned, then suddenly lost the grin when she remembered what had happened to the scats. "I didn't even show you that tank," she said. "Or did you find it yourself? It's in the living room."

I hadn't noticed it on my way through, so the two of us went back to look at it. There wasn't really a hell of a lot to look at. When you've seen one aquarium you've seen them all, when all they contain is water. This particular water may have had enough strychnine in it to kill a lot of people, but it certainly looked innocuous enough.

"I siphoned out the dead fry," she said. "Then I was going to get rid of the rest of the water, but is it safe to pour it down the sink? There's poison in it, after all, and I don't want to wipe out half of Manhattan."

"It would just go in the sewers," I said. "It would probably get completely diluted. But if you don't want to risk it I guess you can let the water evaporate and then throw out the tank."

"Throw out the tank?"

"Well, I don't know much about strychnine. Would it evaporate along with the water? And meanwhile there's the chance someone would drink out of the aquarium. I admit it's not much of a chance, but why take it?"

"Maybe we'd better flush it down the toilet," she said. "I can find out later how to clean the tank so that it's usable again. It won't be destroying the evidence, will it? I have the lab report and everything."

I assured her that it wouldn't be destroying evidence, and the two of us lugged the tank into the bathroom and emptied it down the toilet. And yet, it did take two of us, and if she hadn't been a big strong lady it would have taken three of us, because water is a lot heavier than you might think. After it was empty Tulip sloshed water into it from a bucket and rinsed it out a few times, and then she put it in the closet where it could rest until she found out how to cleanse it thoroughly.

I couldn't see how we had destroyed any evidence, but what I didn't bother to tell her was that evidence didn't make much difference. Granted that she wanted to know who had killed her fish, but with all the evidence in the world we weren't going to take whoever it was to court and prosecute him. I didn't mention this because it might lead her to wonder why she was spending good money to track the villain down, and I didn't want this thought to cross her mind until her check cleared.

When the tank was tucked away in the closet, Tulip heaved a sigh. "That's a lot of exercise," she said. "Not like dancing all night, but all that lifting and toting. I used muscles I don't normally have any call for. Look, I'm all sweated up."

She didn't have to tell me to look. I was already looking. Her tee-shirt was damp now and Beethoven was plastered all over her. I've been apt to envy a lot of people in the course of my young life, but this was the first time I had ever been jealous of a dead composer.

"Just look at me," she said, lifting her arms to show the circles of perspiration beneath them, and then she saw that I was indeed looking at her, and she managed to read the expression on my face, which I guess you didn't have to be a genius to read anyhow, and then she laughed again. "Bourbon and yogurt! On the *rocks*!"

I told her to stop it.

And that was about that. She had a dinner date, and she was going to have to shower and change, but we had time to sit around and talk for a while. She told me a little about some of the names in my notebook but nothing worth recording, or even worth training my memory to retain. She also told me a great deal about herself—how someone had given her a couple of baby guppies when she was eleven years old, and how she had really gotten into fish in a big way until her parents' house was hip-deep in fish tanks, and how in high school she had grown profoundly interested in biology and genetics, and how someday she hoped to make an important contribution to ichthyological knowledge. In the meantime she was dancing naked, making decent money, saving as much of it as she could, and not at all certain where her career should go from here.

"I suppose I could get some sort of institutional job," she said. "At a public aquarium, or preparing specimens for museum collections. I have good qualifications. But I haven't found an opening that turns me on at all, and I'd rather prefer to live in New York, and I can't see myself clerking in some place like Aquarium Stock Company for two-fifty an hour."

There was a lot of conversation which I didn't bother reporting to Haig and won't bother reporting to you because it was trivial. But trivial or not, it was also pleasant, and I was sorry when it got to be time to go.

"Come to the club tonight," she said. "Come around one and you can catch my last set, and you'll get to see Cherry too. You'll want to talk to her, won't you?"

"Sure," I said. "But she might have plans, and—"

"So at least you'll get to see my number, Chip." She grinned hugely. "You wouldn't mind watching me do my dance, would you?"

I took the subway to 23rd and Eighth and walked the few blocks to Leo Haig's house. Wong had waited dinner until my return. He doesn't say much, but he cooks really fantastic Chinese things, and he never seems to dish up the same thing twice. Which is a shame, because there are plenty of dishes I'd like to return to.

I *hope* he throws out the roaches—

We talked business throughout our dinner. Haig has this tendency to imitate Nero Wolfe, and he attempts to avoid it by not making Wolfean rules for himself, like no business at meals and set hours with the orchids—which is to say fish in his case. So we talked, or rather I talked and he gave the appearance of listening, pausing periodically in his eating to ask a question or wipe some hoi-sin sauce from his beard. When the meal was finished we went back into the office and Wong brought the coffee. There was no dessert. There never is at Haig's house. He thinks if he never has dessert he will get thin. So we skipped dessert, as usual, and he opened his desk drawer, the second from the top on the left, and took out a Mars bar and two Mallo Cups. I passed, and he ate all three of them. If he keeps up like this he'll be nothing but skin and bones before you know it.

"Five hundred dollars," he said at one point, between bites, "is a rather large retainer for a case involving the murder of fish."

"It's standard," I said.

"Phooey."

"All right, it's large. It works out to almost five dollars a fish, which is about the going rate for scats, although I don't suppose fry would bring that much, would they? On the other hand she lost a breeding pair, and since they're the only known breeding pair of *Scatophagus Tetracanthus* they might be worth the full five hundred all by themselves. On the other hand—"

"You already said that."

"On the third hand, if you prefer, we're not going to bring the fish back to life even if you *are* a genius, so maybe that's the wrong way to approach it. Look at it this way—"

"Chip."

"Yes, sir."

"I assume you had a reason for setting so high a price."

"Yes. A few of them. First of all, the rent Madam Juana pays you isn't enough to cover our overhead, and I have a vested interest in that overhead since I'm part of it. We can use the money. That's one. Two is I wanted to see if she could write a check for five hundred dollars without batting an eyelash. I watched her closely and she didn't bat a single one of them."

"You were not looking at her eyelashes."

"I'll let that go. The third reason is I thought that a high retainer might shame you into telling her to go swim upstream and spawn. How the hell are we going to find out who wiped out her scats? And where's the glory in it for you if we do? I know you didn't take the case for the money or you would have remembered to *ask* for the money, so you've got to be doing it for the glory, and if you think this is going to make your name a household word like stove and refrigerator and carpet—"

"Chip."

I stopped in midsentence. When he uses that particular tone of voice I stop. I stopped, and he spun around and regarded the Rasboras, and I waited for something to happen.

He spoke without turning from his fish. "I suppose it must be as it is," he said. "The Watson character is expected to lack subtlety. Thus the detective sparkles in comparison to his less nimble-witted assistant."

"You always pick the nicest ways to tell me how stupid I am."

"Indeed. You're quite useful to me, you know, and yet it's remarkable how you can simultaneously ignore subtleties while overlooking the obvious."

"I can also walk down the street while chewing gum."

"I'll accept your word on that." He turned around again and put his feet up, dammit. "Of course you'll go see our client perform tonight."

"All right. If you're determined that she's still our client—"

"I am."

"Then I'll go."

"And you'll interview Miss Bounce after the performance."

"If you say so."

"I do. With whom is Miss Wolinski dining tonight?"

"I don't know. Someone who's luckier than I am. Why?"

"You didn't ask?"

"Sure I asked. She said it wasn't one of the names in the notebook, so I—"

"But she didn't give the name."

"No."

He closed his eyes. I was still there when he opened them, and I don't think the fact delighted him. "You may leave," he said. "I want to read. Could you get me that new Bill Pronzini mystery?" He pointed and I fetched. I asked politely if the book was part of Pronzini's series in which the detective does not have a name.

"He has a name," Haig said. "The name is not revealed to the reader, but clearly the man has a name."

"Well, you know what I mean."

"What Pronzini's detective does not have," he said, "is an assistant." He glared at me, then lowered his eyes to the book. I thought about wishing him goodnight and decided against it.

I went out and killed time. I had a beer at Dominick's and watched the Mets. They were playing the Padres and they lost anyhow. It took some doing. They went into the ninth two runs ahead. Then Sadecki struck out the first two batters and it looked hard to lose. He hit the next batter, and this rattled him so that he walked the next two, at which point Berra yanked him and sent in Harry Parker, who got the batter to hit a slow grounder to Garrett. Garrett fielded it cleanly but didn't throw to first because he couldn't find the ball. It was lost somewhere in his glove. That loaded the bases and upset Parker, who threw the next pitch six feet over Grote's head, cutting the lead to one. That was it for Parker. Berra brought in somebody just up from Tidewater, who made his major league debut by promptly hanging a curve for Nate Colbert. I think the ball's still in the air somewhere over Queens. That made it 5 to 3, and we went down in order in our half of the ninth, and that, to coin a phrase, was the ballgame.

"Jeez, they stink," Dominick said.

I couldn't argue with that. I walked around for a while, and then I went to Treasure Chest, and I guess that brings you up to date, because there I was on the stage and there was a beautiful girl named Cherry Bounce on the stage next to me and she was a hundred percent dead and this was something my ingenuity and intelligence and experience had not prepared me for.

Four

I JUMPED DOWN from the stage, and then I vaulted up onto the bar and slid on the residue of someone's drink. I landed somewhat imperfectly on the customers' side of the bar. A lot of people were moving toward the stage, curious to know what was happening, and a lot of other people were moving toward the door, and the second group were the ones I was concerned with. I did some fancy broken-field running and got to the door ahead of most of them. I planted myself in the doorway with my arms and legs wide and tried to look as substantial as possible.

"Nobody leaves," I said. "A girl has been killed. Nobody leaves until the cops get here."

A couple of men took my word and turned away. I was on the point of congratulating myself on my menacing snarl when a few other guys headed toward me and looked prepared to walk right through me.

"Nobody leaves," I said again, terrified that my voice would crack. They kept right on walking.

Then someone moved up against me from my right, and I turned my head, and it was my friend the door-tender, plaid pants and striped jacket and sky blue shirt and all. He moved into the doorway and I moved over to give him room, and he planted himself there in the identical stance I had taken, but he looked as though he meant it.

"Everybody stay where you are," he said. He didn't speak as loudly as I had. Then again, he didn't have to. The people milled a little, but then they turned back and resigned themselves to the fact that they weren't going anywhere.

"I gotta hand it to you, kid," the doorstop grunted. "You got moxie."

I beamed idiotically for a moment, then ducked back into the club myself. A lot of people were behaving pretty hysterically at this point and I can't say I blamed them much. I hadn't noticed any women in the club—except for Tulip and Cherry and the bar-maid, obviously—but evidently there had been women at some of the back tables, or else someone had hired a batch of women to run into the club and scream when Cherry's body hit the stage. There was plenty of scream-ing, that's for sure.

I managed to find Tulip, who was not contributing to the screaming one bit. At first she looked oddly calm, but then I took a second look and recognized her expression as the kind of calm you get when someone has recently hit you over the head with a mallet.

She said, "She's—"

I was going to let her finish the sentence herself but she just plain stopped. So I finished it for her. "Dead," I said.

"What was it? A heart attack?"

"It was murder."

"But—"

"There's no time," I said. "This must be tied in with the scats and it proves Leo Haig is a lot smarter than I'll ever be but I already knew that. Listen to me. Are you listening?"

She nodded.

"All right. You and I don't know each other. No, the barmaid knows we do. Shit. All right."

"Chip?"

"You don't know anything about Haig. You don't mention anything about fish. You don't even know Cherry was murdered except that's what people have been saying. Are you a good liar?"

"I don't know. I guess so."

"Well, do the best you can. Now all I have to do is figure out a way to get the hell out of here." I looked at the door, and my friend the gorilla was still in place; now that I had taught him not to let anybody out, it was a cinch he wasn't going to let *me* out. I tried to figure out something, and while I was standing there like an idiot a man in a tuxedo came along and supplied the one powerful argument that would have whisked me past the gorilla in nothing flat.

"You!"

He was looking at me, and he was pointing at me, but the expression of absolute fury and indignation on the face of a man I had never seen before in my life convinced me that he had someone else in mind. I figured maybe he was a little cockeyed, and I looked over my shoulder to see who it was that he was furious with, but there was nobody there. Then he was standing right in front of me and his finger would have been touching my nose if either the finger or the nose had been half an inch longer.

"You!"

Tulip said, "Mr. Leemy—"

"Shut up," Leemy said, and my trained memory remembered that one Gus Leemy was the owner of record of Treasure Chest, and it stood to reason, Leemy being in another class entirely from Smith and Jones, that the Leemy with his finger in my face was Gus himself. Tulip said his name again, and he told her brusquely to shut up again, and that inspired exchange gave me a couple of seconds to look him over.

I decided that what he looked like was a bald penguin. The tuxedo, of course, and an absolutely hairless dome atop a long narrow head. He moved like a penguin, too; little jerky motions like old silent movies before they learned how to get the timing right.

"You're not twenty-one," Leemy said.

I opened my mouth and closed it again. Somehow I didn't think another portrait of Alexander Hamilton was going to cut much ice with the man.

"My fucking dancer drops dead on the fucking stage and the place is going to crawl with fucking cops and I need you like a fucking hole in my head. Out!"

"But—"

"Out!" He grabbed me by the arm, tugged me toward the door. He wasn't all that big or strong and at first I stood my ground, and then I remembered that he and I agreed that I should get out of there. At which point I stopped resisting.

He said, "Joint crawling with cops and all I need is trouble with the fucking S.L.A. about my fucking liquor license, all I fucking need, out, you little prick, and don't come back, and—"

I couldn't have agreed with him more, and I could have walked faster if he'd just let go of my arm. But he didn't, and I couldn't have walked fast enough anyway, because we were still maybe a dozen steps from the door when three of four gentlemen in blue uniforms filled the doorway.

"Oh, shit," Gus Leemy said.

The patrolmen mostly stood around and made sure that nobody entered or left the premises. One of them went up on the stage to confirm that Cherry was dead. When he came back down somebody asked if the girl was dead and he refused to commit himself. "We'll let the medical examiner settle that question," he said. I guess Dylan was wrong; some people really do need a weatherman to know which way the wind is blowing.

I did manage one feat while the patrolmen stood around waiting for the heavyweights to reach the scene. I found the phone booth and looked in my pocket for a dime. I only had a quarter, and my ingenuity and experience told me not to waste time getting change. I dropped the quarter and dialed my favorite telephone number, and when Wong Fat answered I told him to wake Haig, and he said he couldn't because Haig hadn't gone to sleep yet. He put the great man on the phone and I talked a little and listened a little and was off the phone by the time the detectives from Homicide, flanked by a couple of other detectives from Midtown West, came plainclothesing their way through the door.

The phone booth was not far from the door they entered. I saw them before they saw me, but not very much before. Just long enough for my heart to sink a little. I recognized them right away, but they needed two looks at me to make the connection. They worked in perfect unison, those two homicide cops in the middle, looking simultaneously at me, looking away, then doing a beautifully synchronized double-take.

"You!" they said. Much as Gus Leemy had said it. And I figured if we were going to stand their trading Gus Leemy lines, I had mine all picked out.

"Oh, shit," I said.

The one on the left was Detective Vincent Gregorio, a tall and dark and handsome number with one of those twenty-dollar haircuts and a suit you'd never find at Robert Hall. The one on the right was Detective Wallace Seidenwall, and I'd decided some time ago that Gregorio liked having him for a partner for the same reason pretty girls like having ugly girlfriends. Seidenwall's suits always looked as though someone else had bought them at Robert Hall, then wore them day and night for a year before passing them on to Seidenwall. I never had trouble remembering his name because he was built like the side of a wall.

The first time I met the two of them was when I discovered the body of a girl named Melanie Trevelyan. The second time I met them was when somebody bombed Madam Juana's whorehouse. That was the memorable day when Haig called them witlings, which was accurate if not diplomatic. The third meeting was in Haig's office, when he unmasked a murderer and presented him to them on a Sheffield platter. You'd think they might be grateful, but you'd be wrong.

If there were two things Seidenwall and Gregorio hated, I was one of them. Haig was the other.

Five

"It was a Mexican standoff," I told Leo Haig. "Gregorio wanted to arrest me and Seidenwall wanted to arrest your client. I was hoping they would arrest us both and lock us up in the same cell, but then I figured you'd have Addison Shivers down there with a writ just when Tulip began to realize that it's hip to be involved with younger men."

Haig grunted. "There are other things in life beside sex," he said.

"I know," I said. "That's the whole trouble. One of the things there is beside sex is coffee. At the moment I'll settle for second best. Is there any?"

Haig picked up a little bell and rang it, and before the vibrations quit Wong entered with a couple of mugs full of hot black coffee. He's extraordinary that way. You hardly ever have to tell him what it is you want.

In this case maybe it wasn't all that extraordinary. It

was six-thirty in the morning and I had been up all night, and while Haig had dozed on the couch waiting for me to turn up he hadn't had anything you'd be likely to call real sleep. Of course we wanted coffee.

By the time I had finished my cup and rung for a refill, I had brought Haig up to date to the point where the cops walked in. I gave him everything reasonably verbatim and he took me back over various points until he was satisfied.

Then I went through my own interrogation. I had gotten off some good lines and I was careful to repeat them all, but since then I've reevaluated them, and while they were nice enough at the time, I don't think I'm going to inflict them on you. I'm not really all that inclined to play smartass with New York's Finest, but those two bring out the wiseacre in me and I have trouble controlling myself. To give you an example of the level of repartee, at one point Gregorio tried a trap question, asking me why I'd been jealous of the girl in the first place, and I said Haig had selected her to crossbreed with one of his fish in the hope that half the offspring would be mermaids and the other half would be Esther Williams. And that was one of my better lines, so now you know why you'll never hear the others.

Haig perked up at that particular line, as a matter of fact. "Then they know about Miss Wolinski's fish?"

"Yes, sir. They were going to find out she had fish, and even the police can add two and two. I told them I

was at the club because I was friendly with Tulip, and
I said the friendship had happened because Tulip had
consulted you as a fellow aquarist about a problem
connected with her hobby."

"Which is not untrue," Haig murmured.

"I know that. I don't lie to the police unless I have
to. Tulip overheard me say this, and she picked up
the ball neatly enough. She said she doesn't know
how good a liar she is. If they grill her I guess she'll
find out."

"And will they grill her?"

"Over and over again. She was Cherry's roommate,
she was a few yards away from her when she was
murdered. They'd have to be crazy not to grill her."

"There's no doubt that Miss Bounce was poisoned?"

"None. I saw the blood on her breast. So did someone else, so the M.E. knew where to look for a wound.
Just a pinpoint puncture."

"And the cause of the puncture was not found."

"No. I looked. The first thing that I thought of was
poison. I thought of it before she hit the ground. God
damn it, I was looking right at her and I never saw
anything hit her. I just saw the blood and then she
reached for herself and started to fall. Christ."

"Chip?"

"I'm all right. When I got up on the stage I was looking for the weapon at the same time that I was determining that she was dead. Not that it was hard to

determine. She was all blue in the face. I forget what that's called. Cyanitis?"

"Cyanosis. And you weren't looking for the weapon. You were looking for the projectile. A gun is a weapon and a bullet is a projectile."

"Well, you knew what I meant."

"My cryptographic ability does not justify your abandoning the English language. You found nothing?"

"Nothing. I didn't know what I was looking for. Something sharp, but that was as far as I got. A dart or a needle or, hell, anything at all. I didn't have much time and of course the lighting was terrible, and if it was something like a needle it could have rolled between the floorboards and disappeared."

"If it's there, the police will find it. Whatever it may be."

"Maybe."

"Absolutely." He took a pipe from the rack and began twisting it apart. The end of the stem broke off inside the shank and he stared at it, sighed, and dropped both pieces into his wastebasket. He looked at me to see if I was going to smirk, and when I didn't he went on. "That is their strength. Scientific methodology, exhaustive investigation. If pressed they could find a needle in a haystack. Certainly they can locate one in a nightclub. Unless the murderer has already removed it."

I thought about that. "He could have," I said. "It must have hit her and bounced off after puncturing her skin, and if he saw it land he'd have had plenty of time to pick it up. I didn't make the world's greatest search for it. I felt it was important to keep as many people inside the place as possible until the police got there."

"You were probably right," he said. He cupped his beard, making sure that all the hairs were the right length. "I gather the murderer could have left before you barred the door."

"Easily. He could have been out the door before Cherry hit the stage, and then he would have had another minute or two while I was checking out the body. A lot of people did leave, I know that much."

"Hardly an admission of guilt on their part. One can readily appreciate the concern of any number of innocent citizens not to have their presence in such an establishment a matter of public record. All those gentlemen who habitually assure their wives that they are working late at the office."

"There were enough of those who didn't get out. When the cops went around taking names, you wouldn't believe the number of John Smiths who turned up. Of course the cops insisted on seeing identification and took down everybody's name and address."

"And you recognized some of the names."

I stared at him, which of course pleased him no end. "How did you know that?"

He waggled a finger at me. "You're still a boy who eats the cake and then the frosting, Chip. You save the best for last. If none of our suspects had been present you would have said so earlier. Who was there?"

I got out my notebook and flipped it open. "I can't say who might have left beforehand. And I can't be sure that I got the names of all the suspects who *were* there, because Seidenwall and Gregorio didn't take me into their confidence. I overheard a few names and I got together with Tulip and she pointed out a couple of people. She didn't know any of them were there until she happened to see them. Incidentally, her dinner date tonight was with a cousin from Chillicothe, Ohio. He came into town on business yesterday morning and flew home after they had dinner at the Autopub. I didn't find out what they had for dinner but I could probably check it out for you."

"Chip."

"Yes, sir. Gus Leemy was there, obviously. I told you how he did his impression of a bald penguin. That's not suspicious because he's always there. Andrew Mallard was there. That's the ex-boyfriend, the one who kept Tulip's apartment so she had to find another one."

"Indeed. And Tulip did not know of his presence beforehand?"

"No. He never talks to her. He usually gets a good table, but what I found out is that there's no such thing as a good table as far as being up close is concerned. The bar is between the tables and the stage. He came alone, of course. Tulip said he always does."

"Did you speak to him?"

"I didn't have a chance. I got a good look at him, though, and I got the impression of a man who goes through life in a fog. He's tall and thin and he'd be taller if he straightened out his spine a little. He walks with a stoop. Oh, and he wears very thick glasses. From where he was sitting, if he shot a dart or something into Cherry, he was probably aiming at Tulip."

"Continue."

"Simon Barckover was there. Tulip didn't know about this, either, but that wasn't unusual either. He drops in occasionally with someone he's trying to convince to book one of his clients. And he usually doesn't give advance warning that he's coming to keep his clients from getting uptight. He was there with a man who books acts for a nightclub in West Orange. I didn't get the name."

"I doubt that it matters."

"Well, I tried, all the same. Barckover's a forty-five-year-old hippie. Embroidered pre-faded jeans, the kind of counterculture clothing you can buy for about two hundred dollars a pair in the East Sixties. A buckskin jacket with fringe that probably cost him double that. Aviator glasses, wears his hair in a Hebro."

"I beg your pardon?"

"It's Tulip's word but I think I like it and I'm going to make it mine. A Hebro. Sort of a Jewish Afro."

"Indeed."

I closed the notebook. "That's it. Just those three, and it wasn't unusual for any of them to be there.

Leemy owns the place, or pretends to. Mallard comes in a lot because he likes to look at Tulip's breasts while he drinks. Barckover had a professional reason for being there. It's possible that there were other suspects there. I don't mean of the ones who ducked out when they had the chance, but besides that. For instance, Mrs. Haskell Henderson might have been there and how would we know it? Tulip's never met her."

Haig sighed. Then he folded his hands, and then he extended his index fingers and played here's-the-church-here's-the-steeple. I got up and looked at some fish.

He said, "The poison. Strychnine?"

"I don't know. They'll have to do an autopsy. What do people look like when they die of strychnine poisoning? Besides dead, I mean."

"The symptoms you described are not incompatible with a diagnosis of strychnine poisoning. It works on the nervous system, the effects are rapid, there's spasmodic paralysis. But it's almost invariably given orally. I suppose it could be used to tip a dart or arrow or whatever projectile was employed." He furrowed his eyebrows. "If it was a poison other than strychnine—"

"Then what?"

He grunted, shook off the question.

"If it was strychnine, then it ties in with the fish. Is that what you mean?"

"No," he said.

"Well—"

"It's tied to the fish in any case," Haig said impatiently. "A young woman comes to see us. Her fish have been deliberately poisoned. Less than twelve hours after she sets foot in this office, her roommate and co-worker is also deliberately poisoned, and under our eyes. Your eyes, at any rate, and you in turn function as my eyes. The connection is undeniable. Anyone who would raise the gray banner of coincidence would—how did that congressman put it? If a mouse walked into the room, he would say that one could not be certain that it was a mouse, that it might well be an elephant with a glandular condition."

It was the other way around; if an elephant walks into the room one says it might be a mouse with a glandular condition. But as much as I like to nitpick with Haig, if only to give him some of his own back, this didn't seem to be the time to pick that particular nit.

Instead I said, "Well, I took it for granted the two things were connected. Obviously. But what difference does it make if it was strychnine both times?"

"Perhaps none. Who else was in the club?"

"The names of all the people whose names didn't ring a bell? God, I don't know. I couldn't run around writing everything down, for Pete's sake. I think most of the men I overheard were from out of town. There could have been a boyfriend or two of Cherry's there. She evidently had a lot of them, former and current.

Tulip wouldn't recognize them either by name or face, so I couldn't say. I know Leonard Danzig wasn't there because Tulip would have spotted him."

"You mentioned a short heavy man who tended the door. A bouncer, I presume."

"Well, he tried to bounce me. And if I hadn't slipped him a ten he would have done it with no trouble. His name is Buddy Lippa. I assume he has an official first name, but all I heard was Buddy."

"Waitresses? Or waiters?"

"Definitely waitresses. Two of them working the tables, and I didn't bother to get their names, but not because I was being stupid. I figured I could get them later from Tulip. Or from Lenny or anywhere else."

"And behind the bar?"

"Her name is Jan and I could probably fall in love with her if I wasn't already committed to Tulip. I understand Tulip doesn't like to play threesies. Leonard Danzig tried to arrange that once and she didn't go for it. But maybe she was just saying that because she was shy, meeting me for the first time and all. After this is over Tulip and Jan and I can get together and work it all out. As a matter of fact—"

"Chip."

I finished my coffee. It was cold, but that was all right. We sat around for a while, and then Haig turned on the news and we had the story, and there wasn't much to it that we didn't already know. They gave

Cherry's real name but they got it wrong, and they said that the police expected to make an arrest very shortly.

Haig grunted and shut off the radio.

"Well, we're out of it," I said. "The police expect to make an arrest at any moment. Of course whoever killed Cherry also killed the fish, so they'll be solving your case for you. Do we give Tulip her check back or not? I'm not sure of the ethics involved."

Haig didn't answer me. After a moment he said, "You'll want to sleep, I suppose. There's a convertible sofa in your room. I've had Wong—"

"There's nothing but a bed and chest of drawers in my room and you know it. If you mean the guest room, that is not my room, and we've been through this enough so that you should have figured it out by now."

He held up a hand. "Please," he said. "The police are not going to apprehend the murderer. Either they will not make an arrest at all or they will arrest the wrong person. That was the seven o'clock news. Sometime between now and noon the police will come here. I want you here when they arrive."

"You're sure they'll come?"

"It's beyond doubt. Wong has made up the bed for you. This does not commit you to living here. You know as much. Get what sleep you can."

"All right."

I got to my feet. He said, "Chip? I'd like to amend a comment I made earlier. Your talents are a very important part of this operation of ours. You performed satisfactorily tonight."

"I was slow getting onto the stage and slow getting to the door."

"Immaterial. You think well on your feet while I think well seated. We work well together. Don't doubt that you're appreciated."

"For Pete's sake," I said. "I'm not used to that kind of talk." He averted his eyes. "I mean, I'll be up for hours wondering what you meant by that. How am I going to get any sleep now?"

As a matter of fact, I did have a tough time getting to sleep. I went so far as to take off my clothes and get under the covers. Then I closed my eyes.

And that was all it took. The next thing I knew Wong Fat was shaking me awake. I made a few horrible noises and buried my face in the pillow but this didn't seem to faze him.

"Police gentlemen here," he said. "Mistuh Haig want you downstairs chop-chop."

I sat up and rubbed my eyes. "What time is it?"

"Is ten-thirty. He want you velly soon, chop-chop."

"Oh, come off it, Wong," I said. "Nobody talks like that. Not even you."

"Is to make innasting character for book you lite," Wong insisted. "Mistuh Haig, he want it just so."

I got out of bed. "Tell him I'll be down in a minute, will you?"

"Ah, so."

"And Wong?"

"Mistuh Chip?"

"Tell him he's a plick."

Six

As I APPROACHED the door I heard Haig telling them that it was no use, that he wasn't going to tell them anything until I was present. Seidenwall sputtered a little at that, and I was tempted to wait out in the hall and let him sputter, but instead I went in and nodded at them and sat down in my chair at the desk. Haig was in his chair across the desk from me and Seidenwall was slumped in the floral wing chair and Gregorio was on his feet. He had changed his suit since I saw him. His partner hadn't.

Haig said good morning, which it clearly wasn't, and I backed him up and wished him a good morning right back. He said he hoped I slept well, and I said it was long on quality if short on quantity, and Seidenwall mentioned a popular organic fertilizer often to be found in stables.

"Now then," Haig said. "What seems to be the matter, gentlemen?"

Seidenwall went purple in the face and squeezed the arms of his chair. Gregorio said, "Look, you silly little butterball, I want some cooperation from you. When I saw this punk who works for you last night I figured you were all wrapped up in this one. I never yet ran into Harrison here without somebody being dead. And what do I get from him? I get a fish story."

"Precisely," Haig said.

"A whole load of crap about how this Tulip broad is just a good friend of his, and he's friends with her because she raises fish and you raise fish and you had a cute little conference about your goddamned fish, and on the strength of that he went to see her dance."

"But that's quite true," Haig said. "Miss Wolinski lost a valuable batch of fish. She wanted me to determine how the fish had perished."

"Yeah, fish." Gregorio looked disgusted. "She even gave me their goddamned names. *Scatophagus tetracanthus.* For the hell of it I looked it up. You know what *Scatophagus* means?"

"Certainly."

"It means eater of excrement. In other words they eat shit, and so does your story."

"It's a misappellation," Haig said dreamily. "The species lives in foul water and subsists on detritus, but I don't believe they actually consume excrement."

"Well, your story does. The fish didn't just die. They were poisoned."

"So it would appear."

"Strychnine," Seidenwall said.

"Strychnine," Gregorio said. "Now who in the hell would dump strychnine into a tankful of fish?"

"An excellent question, Mr. Gregorio. And it was precisely Miss Wolinski's question, which prompted her to consult me. I have as yet been unable to hit on the answer."

Gregorio stared at him. Staring at Leo Haig does you no good whatsoever, but I didn't point this out to Gregorio. There's no point in volunteering information to the police. They never really know what to do with it, anyway.

"Awright," Seidenwall said. "Where does your little pal Harrison get off keeping this all to himself last night?"

"I'm sure I don't know," Haig said. "Chip? Did the police ask you if Miss Wolinski's fish were poisoned?"

"The subject never came up," I said.

"Now wait a minute—"

"Did they mention strychnine? Did they inquire as to whether any professional relationship existed between ourselves and Miss Wolinski?"

"Nope."

"Well then," Haig said. "Gentlemen, I don't understand. You accuse my associate of failing to cooperate. Of prevaricating. Yet he has neither lied nor withheld information. Why should he assume that the death of a group of fish bore any relationship to the death of a topless dancer? Had he even suggested this line of inquiry, no doubt you would have accused him of wasting your time."

They both started calling Haig names. Seidenwall called him a lump of shit while Gregorio called him a fat dwarf. Haig did not seemed ruffled. He took a pipe apart and put it back together again. This time he didn't break it.

Seidenwall said, "The hell, Vinnie. Let's get to the point."

"Right." Gregorio walked over to the desk. He planted himself next to me so that he could glower down at Haig. I was tempted to check out the material of his suit but I restrained myself. "All right," he said. "We could go round and round with this but it's a waste of time. You're too damn cute. You sit on your fat ass and play with your pipes and your fish and talk your way out of everything. But you're covering for a client, dammit, and you're withholding evidence and I want it."

Haig looked at him.

"You know what I'm talking about. Or didn't your little chum tell you? He was sitting right next to the Wolinski broad when she put the dart in her roommate. I'd make it twenty-to-one he saw her do it, but I don't suppose we could ever prove it."

"Indeed."

"Then he was on the stage before the body stopped twitching. That's when he picked up the murder weapon." Haig didn't tell him he meant projectile. "And you can't deny he was on the stage, damn it. A dozen people saw him hop over the bar and onto the stage."

"Why deny it?" I put in. "I told you all that last night. I might have looked around for a murder weapon if I knew she'd been murdered, but how was I supposed to know that? I didn't even know she was dead. That's what I went up onto the stage to find out, and she was. What does that prove?"

"I proves you're a fucking liar," Seidenwall said.

"Harrison has the murder weapon," Gregorio went on. "He's got it and I know he's got it and, damn it, you know he's got it. Some dumb broad raises tropical fish and that makes her okay in your book and you're covering for her. Well, I've got her locked up and I'm going to nail her on Murder One, and if you don't come up with the dart or whatever it was I'll have you and Harrison in the dock on an accessory charge."

"Indeed," Haig said. He heaved a sigh. "Your thesis seems to be that Miss Wolinski murdered Miss Abramowicz."

"You know damned well she did."

"It's curious. First Miss Wolinski poisoned her own fish with strychnine for reasons we cannot begin to explain. Then, no doubt wracked by guilt over what she had done, she hired me to find her out. And, unbalanced at the thought of discovery, she pumped more strychnine into her roommate while my associate sat beside her. Ingenious reasoning, Mr. Gregorio. I applaud you."

"It wasn't strychnine."

"Pardon me?"

"It was curare. The stuff South American Indians put on their arrows."

"I know what curare is," Haig said.

"So she didn't poison her own fish. The two girls hated each other. One of them took a boyfriend away from the other one, so the Abramowicz one got hold of some strychnine—"

"How?" Haig demanded. "Where?"

Gregorio ignored the demands. "—and poisoned Wolinski's fish. Wolinski hired you and you found out Abramowicz did the job. So Wolinski got ahold of some curare and gave Abramowicz the needle, and now you're trying to cover for her."

Haig stood up. This didn't increase his height all that much, but he has a way of getting to his feet that is pretty theatrical. Maybe it's because he stands as infrequently as possible, so that when he finally gets around to it you're really ready for something spectacular.

"Mr. Gregorio. Mr. Seidenwall. I have intimated in the past that I regard you as witlings. I cannot imagine that you are sufficiently mindless to believe the story you have just propounded. It is enough of a mark of your lack of intellect to recognize that you expect me to believe you believe it."

(I don't think they got the gist of that. If you have to read it over a few times yourself, don't feel like an idiot. It's a complicated paragraph. Haig might think you're a witling if you don't get it first time out of the box, but I won't hold it against you.)

"I will not dignify your conjecture with rebuttal," he went on. "Why refute something you already know to be absurd? We have already wasted enough time. Have you taken my client into custody?"

"You're damn right."

"Have you indeed. Mr. Gregorio, there is a blind man who operates a newsstand at the corner of Sixth Avenue and 42nd Street. Perhaps you know him."

"So?"

"Simply this. Were that blind man my client of the moment instead of Miss Wolinski, and had Mr. Harrison been present last night when Miss Abramowicz was murdered, you would have arrested the newsdealer and let Miss Wolinski go. You are trying to put pressure upon me, sir. You are trying to coax me to solve a case which baffles you, and you are trying to force me to do so on your own terms instead of my own. Have you formally charged my client?"

"Not yet."

"Not yet and not ever, as you well know. You have

put her through a profound indignity in order to obtain from me information which I do not have and would not be obliged to give you if I did. You do not know by whom Miss Abramowicz was killed. You do not know the motive. Do you at least know what weapon was employed?"

"Something small and sharp with curare on the tip."

"So you do not know that either. You do not know anything except, I am sorry to say, my address. My inclination is to close up like a clam. First I will volunteer certain information to you. Negative information. Neither I nor Mr. Harrison knows who poisoned Miss Wolinski's fish. Neither of us knows who murdered Miss Abramowicz. Neither of us possesses any factual knowledge not in your own possession. And, finally, neither of us intends to respond further to accusations, charges, questions, or such other irritation as you might be inclined to visit upon us. I have previously merely intimated that you are witlings. I now state it categorically. You are witlings, gentlemen. Your behavior defines the term to perfection. I would urge you to leave my house."

"Now wait a minute—"

"I will wait for eternity if I must. Having admitted you, I cannot legally order you to leave. In the future you shall not be admitted without a warrant. Since you are inside, you may wait here until hell freezes. Such a course of action would be futile for you, but not inconsistent with your character and mental agility. You will excuse me if I do not offer you refreshment."

He rang the bell. Wong came in with his tray. There were two cups of coffee on it. Not four. Just two. Wong gave one to Haig and one to me. He always knows.

They didn't wait for hell to freeze. They tried a couple of questions and bright lines, concentrating on me. "I don't like it," Seidenwall said. "Whenever there's drugs in the picture, this punk turns up."

Gregorio told me to roll up my sleeves.

"Oh, for Pete's sake," I said. "Drugs? Because somebody put strychnine in a fish tank? And what do you mean I turn up when there's drugs involved? What drugs?"

"That hippie chick who took an overdose a while back."

I stared at him, and I started to say something, and Haig said, "Chip. I don't think it's incumbent upon you to play a role in this farce. You need not reply to questions."

"I think you're right," I said. "Do I have to roll up my sleeves?"

"Yes," Seidenwall said.

"No," Leo Haig said.

I took Haig's word for it and sat there sipping coffee. They asked some more questions and got no replies from either of us, so they made some threats and left. I bolted the door after them, and when I got back into the office Haig was already on the phone to Addison Shivers, making arrangements for Tulip's release from custody. Since Addison Shivers is around a hundred and ten years old, I didn't figure he would run around from precinct to precinct himself. But he would make sure someone did it and did it right.

When the phone was cradled again Haig leaned back in his chair. I said, "They're terrific, those two."

"Mmmmm," he said. "I wonder what they meant about drugs."

"Oh, it's just their way of being playful. The first time I met them they asked me to roll up my sleeves and I was wearing a short-sleeved shirt, for Pete's sake."

"I wonder."

"It doesn't mean anything."

"Everything means something," Haig said sleepily. He leaned back and put his feet up and closed his eyes. I didn't object to the gesture now because he was thinking, and a genius is fully entitled to think in whatever position suits him best. He thought for a long time, and when it was questionable whether he was thinking or sleeping I gave up and got some brine shrimp and wheat germ and Tetramin and went around feeding the downstairs fish. I did the other rooms first, then came back to the office. Haig was still leaning back with his feet up and his eyes closed, but at my approach he opened his eyes and fixed them on me.

"The unadulterated nerve," he said. "As if we would willingly shield a murderer. Chip."

"Sir?"

"Could she have done it?"

"Yes, sir. Easily. She made a point of urging me to watch Cherry go into the finale of her act. She could have had a little blowpipe palmed out of sight, and she could have plinked Cherry's tit while I wasn't looking, and Bob's your uncle. There's not a chance in hell that that's what happened, but she could have done it. It would have been a cinch."

"But then why would she have come here?" He sighed. "No. Impossible. Our client is innocent. Someone else committed the murder."

"The same person who dosed the fish with strychnine."

"No. I believe I know who killed the fish. And someone else killed Miss Abramowicz."

"What? You *know* who killed the fish?"

"I believe so. It would be premature to offer conjecture at this point in time. Chip."

"Sir?"

"I never said 'At this point in time' before Watergate. It is a cumbersome cliché. I don't like it. Should I use it in the future, please call it to my attention."

"Sure thing. All part of my job. Feed the fish, clean out the filter traps, change the glass wool and charcoal, chase the murderers, and correct your English. Who killed the fish and how does it tie in with everything?"

He shook his head. "Not now. It would be premature. And we have more pressing concerns. You are going to have to see a great many people and learn as much as you possibly can. Your notebook, please."

Seven

HASKELL HENDERSON OWNED six health food stores, all of them in Manhattan, all located between 72nd Street and Eighth Street. I called one of them and established that he wasn't there, but that he was most likely at the store on Lexington and 38th. I called that one, and they said he was there, and I hung up before he could come to the phone and went out and got a cab.

The store was called Doctor Ecology, and it was a lot larger than the usual watering holes for health nuts. It was the size of a small supermarket, with about half a dozen aisles and shopping carts that you could wheel up and down them while stocking up on gluten bread and soy flour and raw sugar and jerusalem artichokes and tiger's milk and other gourmet treats. At the back there was a lunch counter for people who probably weren't all that hungry in the first place. I hadn't really eaten anything yet that day, and it was close to noon, so I took a stool at the counter and looked at a menu. If only I'd been a rabbit I could have had a hell of a time. I decided that I didn't want anything they had, so I settled for a cup of coffee. Only it wasn't coffee. It was a coffee substitute made by grinding up dandelion roots. The idea was that it wouldn't keep you awake, and it's always seemed to me that the only thing coffee really has going for it is that it *will* keep you awake.

You probably think you can imagine what that dandelion coffee tasted like. Don't bet on it.

I sipped enough of it to know that it was never going to be one of my all-time favorites. I paid for it and left the waiter a large tip because I felt sorry for him. Then I looked around to see if I could pick Haskell Henderson out of the crowd. When that didn't work I asked a cashier if he was around, and she told me he was in his office and pointed out the door that led to it. I knocked on the door and a voice told me to come in.

I walked into a tiny office. Haskell Henderson was standing behind a desk piled so full of invoices and pamphlets and correspondence that the desk top didn't show through anywhere. He was talking on the phone, and the conversation seemed to involve just which brand of brown rice was the most yang, which has something important to do with the macrobiotic diet. I was sort of familiar with the macrobiotic diet because there was a time when I lived with some people in the East Village who were very into it. They ate nothing but brown rice. They also did a lot of speed, which I don't believe is a standard part of the macrobiotic diet, and they talked about all the sensational things they were going to accomplish once they got their heads together. Sure.

While he talked I looked at him. I didn't see anything marvelous, but the fact that he was Tulip's current boyfriend probably prejudiced me against him. He was maybe thirty-five, and he had his hair combed to hide the fact that his hairline was ebbing, and he had a scraggly little goatee to hide the fact that he didn't have much of a chin. He was wearing white jeans and a tee-shirt with "Doctor Ecology" in white letters on a blue background. All the employees wore tee-shirts like that.

He finished his conversation, told the person at the other end of the line to stay healthy, and scuttled out from behind the desk. He thrust out his hand, which I shook, and he gave me a smile designed to show me what great shape his teeth were in.

"Well now," he said. "Haskell Henderson. What can I do for you?"

"My name is Harrison," I said, "and I work for Leo Haig."

"Leo Haig. Leo Haig. Let me see. Dew-Bright Farms? Over in Jersey? I've heard good things about your vegetables."

"Leo Haig the detective," I said.

"Detective?"

I nodded. "Mr. Haig is working for Tulip Willing. Or Thelma Wolinski."

He looked at me suspiciously. "Why would Tulip need a detective? She's not jealous. Wait a minute. Just *wait* a minute now. You're not working for Tulip."

"Mr. Henderson—"

"You're working for my wife," he said, pointing his finger at me. At least it didn't come as close to my nose as Gus Leemy's finger. "You're working for my wife," he said again. "Well, get this straight, fella. I don't know any Tulip Willing, or whatever you said her name was, whoever she may be, and—"

"Shut up."

I don't know why I said that. As far as that goes, I don't know why it worked. Maybe nobody had ever told Haskell Henderson to shut up before, and maybe he didn't know how to relate to it. He opened his mouth, and he closed it, and he stared at me.

I said, "Cherry Bounce was murdered last night."

"Oh, Christ. Yeah, I heard about that. Somebody killed her in the middle of her act. They get the guy yet?"

"They made an arrest. But they didn't get the killer, and the person they got isn't a guy. It's Tulip."

"They arrested Tulip? Jesus, that's ridiculous. I don't get it."

"Well, that's why Tulip hired a detective," I said. "She doesn't get it either, and she's not crazy about it. I want to ask you some questions."

"Why me?"

"Because you're Tulip's boyfriend, and because—"

"Whoa!" He displayed his teeth again and the light glinted on them. "Tulip's boyfriend? You gotta be kidding, fella. I'm a happily married man. Oh, I see Tulip from time to time, no question about that. When a man keeps himself in good physical shape he's got all this energy, he has to find an outlet for it. But Tulip's just one of the girls I see from time to time. It's nothing heavy, you understand? Just a friend, that's all. A casual friend with whom I have an enjoyable physical relationship. You don't want to make a whole big deal out of it."

What I wanted to do was play a tape of this speech for Tulip. Why was she wasting her time on this playboy when I was available? I said, "Look, your wife didn't send me. Honest."

"So?"

"So don't make speeches about how you relate to Tulip like a sister. That's not the point. You're her friend, and you were at the Treasure Chest last night, and—"

"The hell I was!"

I did my best to look confused. I even scratched my head, mainly because I've seen so many people do it when they're confused, especially in movies. The only time I normally scratch my head is when it itches. "That's funny," I said. "According to the information we have, you were at Treasure Chest until just before the time of the murder."

"Well, that's bullshit," he said. He reached into a jar on his desk and stuffed a handful of things into his mouth. They looked like newly hatched fish, little spherical bodies and long stringy tails. (I found out later that they were alfalfa sprouts.) He munched them and said, "I don't know where the hell you heard that. Where did you hear it, anyway?"

"You got me. Mr. Haig said that was his information, but I don't know who told him. Where were you last night, then? Because when I tell Mr. Haig his information was wrong, he'll want to know where you were."

He told me what I could tell Haig to do. It was something I've often wanted to tell Haig to do, as a matter of fact. "I don't have to account for my movements to Leo Haig," he said. "That's for damn sure."

"You don't have to," I agreed. "But, see, the police don't really know anything about you, and if Mr. Haig doesn't have any other way of finding out where you were, he'll let them know about you and let them ask you the same question. If Haig is satisfied, he wouldn't have any reason to mention your name to the police. After all, they're not his clients. Tulip is his client."

I watched his eyes while I delivered this little set piece. There was a moment when he contemplated a show of righteous indignation, but then his eyes shifted and I could tell he knew it wouldn't wash. "Oh, the hell with it," he said. "I have nothing to hide.

As a matter of fact, I was home last night. I was watching television. Do you want to know what programs I saw?"

"Not particularly, but maybe the Neilson people would be interested. Well, that's no problem, then. You were home watching television so that lets you off the hook."

"What hook? You don't suspect me of killing Cherry, do you?"

"Of course not," I said. "How could you? You were home watching television."

"Right."

I started toward the door, then turned around. "While I'm here," I said, "could you tell me a little about Tulip and Cherry? There's a lot I don't know, and since I know you're not a suspect I would be able to rely on what you tell me. It won't take too much of your time."

He wasn't tickled with the idea but he liked the notion of not being a suspect. I asked him a lot of questions and he answered them and I made some notes in my notebook. His chief slant on both of the girls was nutritional. Tulip ate a lot of garbage, he said. Nature had given her a spectacular physique and she was taking a chance of ruining it because she actually ate meat and fruit that had been sprayed and a lot of other no-nos. He had tried to interest her in nutrition but so far it hadn't taken. Cherry, on the other hand, was far more open to new ideas. The impression I got was that he liked Cherry more than he liked Tulip, probably because she was dumb enough to pay attention to him, but he didn't like having Cherry around that much because when he stole over there for an afternoon all he really wanted to do was crawl into the feathers with Tulip, who turned him on something wonderful.

No, he didn't know anyone who would want to kill Cherry. No, he didn't know anyone who had anything against Tulip, either. I slipped in an oblique reference to Tulip's fish and he didn't seem to have strong feelings about them one way or the other. Instead he turned them into nutritional propaganda.

"She knows nutrition is the secret of conditioning," he said. "That's how she gets the breeding results she does. Plenty of live foods. Everything raw. Nothing cooked. She even knows to mix kelp and wheat germ into their formula. My God, they eat a better diet than she does! If she ate what she gives the fish, she'd be in fantastic shape."

If she were in any better shape, I thought, she'd be capable of turning on statues. I was beginning to understand why Tulip had offered me a bourbon and yogurt. It was probably Haskell Henderson's favorite cocktail.

"I guess that's it," I said finally. "Thanks very much for your cooperation, and I'm glad to know you were home watching television last night. That's one name off the list."

"Well, it's not the kind of list I'd want to be on."

"I don't blame you." I gave him my no. 3 warm smile. "Mr. Haig will just ring up your wife and confirm your story, and then we'll be all set."

I would probably respect myself a lot more if I didn't get such a kick out of doing things like that. I mean, I couldn't feature old Haskell as the killer. If he wanted to do somebody in he'd probably poison them with refined sugar and synthetic vitamins, not strychnine or curare. But we still had to know what he was doing last night, and anybody who'd believe the television story has probably already bought the Brooklyn Bridge several times over.

It was fun to watch him. He made the kind of noise in his throat that you make when you get a shirt back from the laundry and button the collar and find out it wasn't Sanforized. Then he took six deep breaths and said, very very quietly, "You can't call my wife."

"Why not?" I grinned. "Oh, sure. You don't want her to know anything about Tulip, right?"

"That's right. She probably suspects I . . . uh . . . see other women. But to have it thrown in her face, and the fact that a girl I know is peripherally involved in a murder case—"

"You don't have a thing to worry about."

"I don't?"

"Not a thing. Mr. Haig is very discreet. The way we'll do it, see, is we'll call up and pretend we're a television survey. Ask her what programs she was watching last night. Then we'll ask if anyone else in her family was also watching television, and she'll say you were, and—"

"She won't say that."

"Oh?"

"I wasn't actually *watching* television. I was in the other room, you see, so she'll say she was the only one *watching* the set, and—"

"We'll ask if other family members were home but weren't watching. Mr. Haig knows all the angles, Mr. Henderson."

"Uh."

I put a little steel into my voice. Or maybe it was brass. "*All* the angles," I said.

"Uh—"

"Where does your wife think you were last night?"

He went for the alfalfa sprouts like a drunk for a drink. He munched and shuddered. "Meeting with the owner of a rival store to discuss a possible merger."

"That's a pretty good line. I don't suppose you can use it too often but it has a nice ring to it. What time did you get to Treasure Chest and what time did you leave?"

"I wasn't there!"

"Where were you? And don't tell me you were with one of the other girls with whom you have a warm physical relationship and you can't drag her name into it because she's respectable. Don't even try that one on."

He met my eyes. "Jesus," he said. "You're just a kid."

"I've had a hard life. What did you do last night?"

"I went to a movie."

"All by yourself, of course."

"As a matter of fact, yes."

I had the notebook open. "What movie?"

"I don't know."

"Oh, come on."

"I don't know the name of it. It was a pornographic movie, one of those, you know, one of those X-rated pictures. I don't remember the title and I can't tell you the plot because it didn't have one. They never have a plot. And of course I went to it alone because who goes to those things *with* somebody? Shit. I thought you believed me about watching television." He got another hit from the jar of sprouts. "I guess I don't have much of an alibi," he said miserably. "Do I?"

Now the next thing that happened is something I never bothered to recount to Haig. I hadn't planned to recount it to you, either, and if you want to skip right on ahead to the beginning of the next chapter, I wouldn't blame you a bit. The following sequence has nothing whatsoever to do with the annihilation of Tulip's fish or the murder of Tulip's roommate, not so far as I can see. Of course if you're into cosmic tides and karmic things and like that, and if you can grok the concept that all things are intimately bound up in one another, then maybe you can justify including the following in this book. I can't, but I don't have much choice in the matter.

What happened was this: I left Haskell Henderson at Doctor Ecology at Lexington and 38th, and I decided to head over to Simon Barckover's office in the Brill Building. But in the meantime I remembered that a friend of mine lived on 37th Street between Third and Second, which wasn't all that far out of my way, and I remembered that I hadn't seen her in a long time, and I remembered what it had been like the last time I had seen her.

So I went over there.

On the way I stopped at a florist's and bought a dollar's worth of flowers. I don't know what kind of flowers they were. (I don't think it matters.) I carried them for a block and remembered that I was going to see Ruthellen, and there was just no way I could walk in there carrying flowers. I didn't really know what to do with them. I mean, you have to be pretty much of a callous clod to stuff a fresh bouquet of flowers into a trash can. I stood there feeling slightly stupid, and then I saw one of the oldest ladies in the world walking one of the oldest dachshunds in the world, and I gave her the flowers. (The lady, not the dachshund.) I walked quickly on while she was still instructing God to bless me.

I couldn't take flowers to Ruthellen because that wasn't the kind of relationship we had. Her problem, which she had laid out for me early on, is that she can't respond at all to people who are nice to her. She's not into whips and chains or anything, but she suffers from what her shrink calls "low estimate of self," and thus she's only turned on by people who despise her. I don't despise her, but I'm willing to pretend to, and it's not hard for me to be aloof and never call her and just drop in on her now and then because, to tell you the truth, she doesn't do all that terribly much for me and I really don't want to get very heavily involved with anybody quite as sick as she is. So maybe I *do* despise her, come to think of it, and maybe that's why she enjoys seeing me.

(Not that it matters. None of this matters at all. That's the whole point.)

I rang her bell. Her voice over the intercom asked who it was. "Chip," I snapped. She asked again. "Chip Harrison," I snarled. She buzzed and I opened the door and climbed two flights of stairs.

She was waiting in the doorway of her apartment. She's about twenty-five, maybe a little older, with a surprisingly good complexion considering that she hardly ever leaves her apartment during daylight hours except for her weekly visit to the shrink. She keeps her shades drawn day and night. She has this thing about daylight. She and the shrink are working on it, she's told me. I don't think they're making much progress, either of them.

"Haven't seen you in ages," she said.

I shrugged. "Been busy."

"Come on in. Can I get you something? A drink?"

"Haven't got time," I said. I sort of swaggered into her apartment and sat down in the comfortable chair. (There's only one.) Ruthellen sat on the couch in a nest of pillows and lit a cigarette.

"Put it out," I said.

"The cigarette?"

"I don't like the smell."

"All right," she said, and put it out. One of the reasons I see her as infrequently as I do is that I don't really like to be a total bastard with a woman. And what I especially don't like is that I can occasionally get into it, and that's a little scary, if you stop to think about it.

(Not that any of this has anything to do with Tulip and her fish and her roommate.)

"Well," she said. "So what's new?"

"Nothing much."

"You don't feel like talking?"

"No."

"That's cool. We'll just sort of sit around and relax. Sure I can't get you anything?"

I grunted. It was a grunt Haig would have been proud of. I sat back and looked at Ruthellen, who, while not the best-looking woman in the world, was by no means the worst. She's tall, about five-eight or so, and very thin, but not so much so that you'd mistake her for Twiggy. Her hair is a dirty blond. Literally, I'm afraid; she doesn't wash it too often. She doesn't do much of anything, really, which is another of the things she and the shrink are supposed to be working on. What she does is sit in her apartment, live on things like Rice Krispies and candy bars—you wouldn't believe how little she and Haskell Henderson would have in common—and cash the monthly check from her father in Grosse Pointe. The check pays for the rent and the Rice Krispies and the candy bars and the shrink, and since that's about all she has to do in life, that's about all she does.

"Chip?"

I looked at her.

"Would you like me to do anything?"

"Take your clothes off."

"Okay," she said.

I could have said *Take your robe off* because a robe was all she was wearing. She took it off and put it on the couch. Then she turned to face me, her hands at her sides, and stood still as if offering her body to me for inspection. Her small breasts were flushed, the nipples erect. She was excited already. So was I, in an undemanding sort of way, but I didn't let it show. I had to go on being Mr. Casual because that was what was turning her on.

"Chip—"

"You could go down on me," I suggested.

"Okay. Do you want to come to bed?"

"Right here's good. You could like kneel on the floor."

"Okay."

And she did. I sat there, Mr. Cool, while she knelt in front of me and unzipped my zipper and, like Jack Horner, put in her hand and pulled out a gland. "Oh, he's so strong and beautiful," she said, talking to it. "Oh, I love him so. Oh, I want to eat him up."

And she did.

It's all we ever do. And it's all according to the same ritual—she always invites me to bed and I always tell her to kneel in front of me like a servant girl, and she always does, and I'll tell you something. Maybe the repertoire is limited, but she certainly plays that one piece perfectly. She doesn't do all that much, Ruthellen, but what she does she does just fine.

Afterward she sat back on her haunches, grinned, wiped one elusive drop from the tip of her chin with the tip of her forefinger, and told me she was glad I had come. She wasn't the only one. "I like it when you drop by," she said. "It gets lonely here."

"You should get out more."

"I guess. The shrink says we're making progress."

"Well, that's good, I guess."

"I guess."

"Well, I'll, uh, see you."

"Take care, Chip."

"Yeah, you too."

Okay.

I feel I owe you an explanation. You're probably wondering why the hell that episode was dragged in out of the blue and thrust in front of your eyes. Of course it took place during the time we were working on this case, but lots of things take place that I don't plague you with. I don't mention every time I go to the toilet for instance. Which is not to say that seeing Ruthellen is like going to the toilet. Except, come to think of it, it is, sort of.

Okay.

When I wrote this book, the Ruthellen bit wasn't in it. And then I got a call from Joe Elder, who is my editor at Gold Medal.

"Like the book," he said. "But there's a problem."

"Oh."

"Not enough sex."

"Oh."

"I'm sure you can think of something."

I argued a lot, but I didn't get anyplace. "We're not in business to sell books," he said. "We're selling hard-ons. Hard-ons sell books. You need a sex scene fairly early on in the book to hook the reader's attention and rivet his eye to the page."

Well, that's why the Ruthellen bit is in. I mean, it did happen, so I suppose it's legitimate. But I'm not really happy with it, and I'd be much happier if Mr. Elder would change his mind and cut it out after all, and—

Oh, the hell with it. Let's get back to the story.

Eight

SIMON BARCKOVER'S OFFICE was in the Brill Building at 1619 Broadway. I went into the lobby and found his name on the board while half the musicians and performers in America walked past me. I rode up to the seventh floor in an elevator I shared with two men carrying saxophones and one swarthy woman toting a caged parrot. I got off and found a door with a frosted glass window labeled *Simon Barckover—Artists' Representative*. There was a buzzer. I pressed it, and a female voice told me to come in.

A girl with red hair and freckles smiled at me from behind a green metal desk that almost matched her eyes. She asked if she could help me. "My name is Harrison," I said, "and I work for Leo Haig. I believe Mr. Barckover is expecting me."

"Oh, yes. You called earlier."

"That's right."

She glanced at the phone on her desk. One of its four buttons was glowing. "He's on a call right now. Won't you have a seat?"

"Thanks but I'll stand."

She took a cigarette from a pack on her desk. "I guess you want to see him about Cherry," she said. "That was a shock. It was really terrible."

"Did you know her? I guess you must have, working in this office."

"I've only been here a couple months."

I looked at her for a moment. "I've seen you before," I said. "You were there last night."

"I was working there. Sometimes if I have a free night I do substitute waitress work in some of the clubs that book a lot of acts through Mr. Barckover. Mostly as a favor, but the extra money helps. Some places you get really decent tips."

"Do they tip well at Treasure Chest?"

"They didn't last night. I've only worked there a couple times and actually they never tip well there. They figure they're being taken, you know, paying such high prices for such rotten drinks, and then there's a cover charge at the tables, so they take it out on the poor waitress by leaving her next to nothing. Last night most of the people didn't even pay their checks in the confusion and everything. But I don't like clubs like Treasure Chest. I just did it last night as a favor to Mr. Barckover."

"Is he a good man to work for?"

Her hesitation answered the question for me. "Well, the pay isn't great," she said. "He's a nice man. He loses his temper a lot but that's because he's in such a high-pressure business. And he's very tolerant. He doesn't get uptight if I smoke dope or like that, and we have an agreement that I can take off whenever there's an audition I want to check out."

"You're in show business?"

"Let's say I'm going to be in show business. I'm a singer. So far nobody's in a rush to pay me money to sing, but I'll make it. Someday you can hear me at the Persian Room of the Plaza."

"I'll take a ringside table."

"You'd better make your reservations now. My opening's going to be sold out months in advance." The green eyes twinkled. "That's why I'm working for Mr. Barckover. He may not be the best agent in the business, but you get a real inside view of things working in an office like this. It's not just making contacts, although that doesn't hurt. It's learning how the business works and how to make your own openings."

I considered telling her that if her voice was as pretty as the rest of her she had nothing to worry about. But in a job like that she'd probably heard every line in the world, and mine was neither all that original nor all that terrific. While I hunted for a way to revise it, the little light on the phone went off.

"I'll tell him you're here," she said, and did. "He see you now," she said. "Right through that door."

I went right through that door. Barckover took a bite out of a sandwich and motioned me toward a seat, chewing furiously. He washed it down with a swig of coffee from a styrofoam container, bit a chunk out of a jelly doughnut, swallowed some more coffee, then lit a half-smoked cigar and leaned back in his chair. It was one hell of a change from Haskell Henderson and the alfalfa sprouts.

So was the conversation. Barckover didn't have to try hiding his presence at Treasure Chest from me because the police already knew about it, and he had a bonafide business reason for being there. The police had already pumped him dry. He'd agreed to see me because he couldn't very well refuse to, since Tulip was his client, but this didn't make him enthusiastic about it. He figured it was a waste of time. Actually more of my time than his got wasted, because he went ahead taking calls during the course of our interview, telling clients that he didn't have anything for them, telling club owners how sensational his clients were. The interruptions were a nuisance but there wasn't much I could do about it.

"I been over this with the police five or six times already," he said. "I was off in the back with this spastic prick from New Jersey. Like I only looked at the stage every ten minutes or so to make sure somebody was on it. You don't know what this business is like, man. After a few years you get so sick of tits and asses that the only way you can get a hard-on is if your woman wears clothes to bed. I never even saw Cherry take her fall. I heard the commotion and I looked up and I couldn't see anything by then because she was lying down and out of sight. I didn't see anybody do anything suspicious. I didn't even think to look for anything suspicious. I figure she fainted from popping too many pills or else she had a bad heart or something. What was it, something pygmies put on darts?"

"Something like that," I said. "Did Cherry take a lot of drugs?"

"For all I know she never even dropped an aspirin. Just going on generalities. Most of the go-go dancers and the topless-bottomless chicks do uppers. All that moving around and all those geeks gaping at them and it gets to them, and a little dexie straightens everything out and they can prevail, they can maintain, if you dig it. Like Lennie Bruce, baby, you got to be on top of it in order to get it out."

I had already been thinking of Lennie Bruce. One line of his in particular. He said there's nothing sadder than an old hipster.

I asked what Cherry was like.

"A comer," he said. "That kid started with nothing. She showed me some pictures of herself taken four, five years ago. Nothing. Big nose, flat in the chest. Not a pig but you'd never look at her twice."

"Cherry?"

He flicked the ash from his cigar. "Plastic surgery," he said. "Her old lady died and left her a couple of K's, no fortune, just of couple of K's, and she went and spent the whole bundle putting herself together. New nose, a trim job for the ears, silicone for the tits, a little of this, a little of that. Changed her name from something nobody can pronounce to Cherry Bounce. Great little name. Usually I pick names for them because most of these girls, they aren't too long in the imagination line. Cherry already had her name picked out when I got ahold of her."

"Did you pick out Tulip's name?"

He shook his head. "Nobody picks out anything for that one. She's smart, you got to hand it to her. Smart, well-educated, the whole bit. I'll tell you something, I think she's too fucking smart for her own good. With the face and body she's got she could have a future in this business. But she won't put out."

"I thought you didn't really have to do that anymore."

"Huh?"

"Put out."

He waved the cigar impatiently. "I don't mean sexual. I mean give out with everything you've got. Take the singing lessons, take the dancing lessons, make all the auditions, cultivate the right people.

Cherry took the trouble. She put out. Tulip, she's got so much going for her, and all she wants to do is coast on what she's got. Pick up the easy bread showing her tits to the visiting firemen and waste all her time with those fucking fish."

"Well, that's her career."

"Career?" He looked at me as though I was an ambulatory psychotic. "You call that a career? Siphoning shit out of fish tanks? What's she gonna make, fifteen K a year running some fucking museum? You call that a career? There's chicks clearing that much a week in Vegas that haven't got half the equipment that girl has."

"But that's not what she wants."

"This year it's not what she wants. Five years from now she'll be Assistant Fish Librarian in East Jesus, Kansas, and that's when she'll realize what she wanted all along was a career in show business. And by then it'll be too late."

I turned the conversation back to Cherry and tried to learn more about her personal life. Barckover turned out to be a less than perfect source. At one point he said that an agent was always in the middle, he was the one with the shoulders that everybody cried on, but Cherry evidently either didn't cry or found other shoulders. He didn't know much of anything about the men in her life, and in his opinion she had been murdered by some sort of weird pervert who got a thrill out of killing strange girls. "You watch it," he said. "There's gonna be a string of hits like this, a Jack the Ripper type killing topless dancers. Probably a religious fanatic." Evidently he didn't know that Tulip's fish had been poisoned, which poked a few holes in the Ripper theory.

An admirable thing about Cherry, according to Barckover, was that she never got seriously involved with any individual male. "Her career always came first," he said. "You get chicks who get hung up on one guy, and I get 'em a week in the mountains and they don't want to leave the guy, so either they pass up a gig or they take it and then they're lousy because they spend all their time pissing and moaning about being lonely. Not Cherry. She knows the priorities. If she's playing house and I get her two weeks in Monticello she goes without a second thought. There's always some dude around to go to bed with, but there aren't always jobs growing on trees."

(He would have been proud of a girl I know named Kim Trelawney. For a while we were almost living together, and she got signed for the ingenue part in a road company version of *The Estimable Sailor*, and although she may have shed a tear or two, off she went. That had been three months ago, and she was still treading the boards in places like Memphis, and we didn't bother writing to each other, and by the time she came back I had the feeling we wouldn't have much to say to each other. It had been a long three months, let me tell you, and maybe that was a contributing factor to the way I reacted to Tulip, but I have to say I'd have probably gone just as bananas over her anyway, to be perfectly honest.)

I asked him about some of the people on our suspects list, and others who had been around Treasure Chest when Cherry was murdered. He had never heard of Haskell Henderson. He'd met Andrew Mallard while Mallard and Tulip were living together, and he said that in his book Mallard was a total feeb. His word, not mine. He'd been delighted when Tulip and Mallard split up.

He knew Leonard Danzig by sight and reputation and could not recall having seen him at the club. And he was surprised to know that Danzig had been keeping company with Cherry. "He's no good," he said. "He's trouble."

"What does he do for a living?"

"You hear lots of things," he said.

"Would you happen to remember any of them?"

"A little of this, a little of that. He plays angles, he hangs with some heavies. I don't know what he does but if it's honest I'll spread it on toast and eat it." He hesitated for a moment. "If he had a beef with a chick, he wouldn't get fancy with poison darts. I don't even think he'd kill her. Maybe he'd beat her up. Or with a beautiful girl like Cherry he'd do something like throw acid on her or cut her so it would leave a scar. That's more his style."

I didn't get a whole lot more than that. If Cherry was having trouble with Helen Tattersall, the downstairs neighbor, Barckover didn't know about it. He had never met Glenn Flatt, Tulip's ex-husband, and didn't know anything about him. He was on nodding terms with Buddy Lippa, Leemy's bouncer and gatetender, and said only that Lippa was a former boxer, a good club fighter who did a decent job of keeping order in the joint. He got evasive when I asked about Leemy, and when I probed to find out who really owned the nightclub he made it obvious that he didn't want to carry that particular ball any further. I asked if either Leemy or Lippa made a practice of making passes at the hired help. He assured me they were both happily married men, which didn't strike me as an answer to the question I had asked, but I let it go.

He didn't know the other waitress or the barmaid, and I didn't ask him about his own secretary because I figured it would be more fun to ask her myself. I wound up the session with Barckover and went into the outer office and perched on the corner of her desk, notebook in hand. "I'm playing detective," I said. "Mind if I ask a couple of questions?"

She grinned. "You mean you're going to grill me? I already told you everything I know."

I told her we'd just go over a couple of things, and we did. I didn't learn much. I found out that the other waitress was named Rita and that was all she knew about her. Jan the barmaid was a regular at Treasure Chest, but my green-eyed friend hadn't had much contact with her except to order drinks and get change. She hadn't seen anything suspicious, hadn't recognized anybody except for Barckover and the people who worked at the club, and she knew nothing about Cherry's private life.

"There's something else," I said. "How am I going to catch you at the Persian Room if I don't know your name?"

She smiled. She didn't show me as many teeth as Haskell Henderson, but they looked better on her. "It's Maeve O'Connor," she said. I made her spell her first name and she did. She also told me it was Irish, but I could have figured that part out by myself. Then she pointed out that she didn't know my first name, so I supplied it, and then I told her I'd better take down her phone number.

"Is that what detectives always do?"

"Not always," I said.

"You could reach me through the office."

"But what if a case starts to break in the middle of the night and I need to check something with you? Mr. Haig would give me hell if I didn't have your number."

She gave it to me and I wrote it down. Then we looked at each other for a minute or two, and I could feel myself beginning to fall in love, which is something I probably do more readily than I should. I would have enjoyed perching on her desk for the rest of the afternoon, but Haig had given me a million things to do and there wasn't all that much time to do them in. I said I guessed I'd better be going, and she said "Goodbye, Chip," and I said, "I'll see you, Maeve," and that was that.

I called the advertising agency where Andrew Mallard worked and got a secretary who said that he was away from his desk. I asked when he would be likely to return to his desk and she said she didn't know. I pressed a little, and it turned out that he hadn't been at his desk all day, that he in fact had evidently taken the day off. I don't know why she couldn't come right out and tell me this straight out, but I guess when you work in advertising you get in the habit of doing things obliquely.

I tried Mallard at his home number and the line was busy. I looked at my watch and saw that it was almost three and remembered that I hadn't had anything to eat all day except for a sip of dandelion coffee substitute. I realized that I had to be hungry. I don't know if this would have occurred to me if I hadn't happened to look at my watch, but once I did I was starving. I found a luncheonette down the block and had a hamburger and three glasses of milk and a cup of coffee. I decided not to look at my watch again because it might remind me how little sleep I had had and I wanted to be awake when I talked to Mallard. Except that I wasn't destined to talk to Mallard. I called him after I'd finished my meal and the line was busy again, and I decided it wasn't the usual sort of busy signal, and I called the operator and asked her to check the line for me. She went into a huddle and came back with the news that the phone was off the hook. (What she actually said was that the instrument's receiver was disengaged, and it took me a second or two to translate it.) That had been my guess, and I decided Mallard had been up half the night with the police and the other half brooding, and now he was taking the day off and having himself a nap.

There's a way the operator can make the phone ring even when it's off the hook, and I considered telling her something about it being a matter of life and death, but they probably hear that line all the time and I didn't think I was likely to get the right note of conviction into my voice. Then too, if Mallard was sleeping it off he probably wouldn't welcome my making a bell ring in his apartment.

The next name on my list was Glenn Flatt, Tulip's ex-husband and current friend. He worked at Barger and Wright Pharmaceuticals in Huntington, Long Island. I got the number from Information and placed the call. The switchboard at Barger and Wright put me through to a man who told me that Flatt was in some laboratory or other and couldn't be disturbed. He asked me if I wanted to leave a number, so I left Haig's.

I didn't have a number for Leonard Danzig, and from what I'd heard about him I decided I wanted to take my time approaching him. Mrs. Haskell Henderson—I still didn't know her first name—lived on the other side of the Hudson. I would eventually want to see her in person, and I'd have to do that during the day when there would be no chance of running into Mr. Wheat Germ himself.

Helen Tattersall was on my list. I had no idea what questions to ask her, but sooner or later I would have to get a look at her, if only to see whether I had spotted her at the club. Tulip's building was in the neighborhood; I could just walk over there and invent a story.

Except that I didn't really want to. Treasure Chest was also in the neighborhood, and Tulip had said that they were open afternoons so that businessmen could stop and goggle at some breasts before heading home to their wives. I wasn't sure that I wanted to look at breasts, but I had to talk to Gus Leemy and he could give me a line on the other waitress and supply

Jan's last name and address. He could also pin my arms behind my back while Buddy Lippa beat me to a pulp.

I decided to chance it.

Nine

"THEY DIDN'T BEAT me up," I said. "What they basically did was ignore me. I had a lot of trouble making them believe I was a detective. They thought I wanted the girls' names because I was trying to make out with them, for Pete's sake."

"They seem good judges of character," Haig murmured.

I ignored that. "The barmaid is Jan Remo. She's been working there for almost a year. She's divorced and has a two-year-old kid. The other waitress—not Maeve—is named Rita Cubbage. She just started there about a week ago. I can see them both late tonight if I'm awake because they'll be working their usual shifts."

"The club will be open, then? In spite of the tragedy?"

"Leemy doesn't think it's a tragedy. He thinks it's a

bonanza. He's got a sign in the window that you'd love. *'See the stage where Cherry Bounce was murdered! See the show so hot it might kill you!'* "

"You're making this up."

"I am not."

"Heavens," Haig said.

We were in his office. It was almost five-thirty and I had just finished summing up my day in my inimitable fashion. I had wanted to rush my report so that I could see Tulip, who had finally been sprung from jail by one of Addison Shiver's underlings and had been conveyed directly to Haig's house after a quick stop at her apartment to shower and change her clothes and feed her fish. Haig had spent about an hour grilling her, and then when I got back I hardly had time to say hello before he'd banished her to the fourth floor so that he could hear my report privately.

She hadn't seemed to mind the banishment—she'd been itching to study Haig's operation up there—but I minded. So I tried to hurry my report but Haig wasn't having any. He made me go over everything in detail and then he sat there with his feet up and I wanted to yell at him.

I said, "So far I'm putting my money on Haskell Henderson. His motives aren't entirely rational, but no one who eats like that is going to behave rationally. You wind up with alfalfa on the brain. Here's what happened. He resented the fact that Tulip's fish ate a better diet than she did. He kept giving her wheat germ and she kept feeding it to the fish and this infuriated him. He figured if he poisoned her fish she'd have to eat the wheat germ herself because there wouldn't be any fish to feed it to and she wouldn't want to let it go to waste. So he made himself some strychnine. I looked up poisons in the encyclopedia, incidentally. Strychnine and curare are both neurotics, which would give them something in common with old Haskell."

"That means they act on the nervous system."

"I know what it means. I was making a funny. I learned that strychnine is extracted from the seeds and bark of various plants. Henderson's got seeds and bark of everything else at Doctor Ecology, so why not *Strychnos Nux-Vomica*? I've been training my memory, that's how come I remember the name of the plant. I hope you're proud of me. He extracted the strychnine and poisoned the fish."

"Phooey."

"Is that all you're going to say? I thought it was a brilliant theory."

He raised his eyebrows. "And Miss Abramowicz? Why did he murder her, pray tell?"

"Give me a minute. I'll come up with something."

"Bah. This is childish. Call Miss Wolinski and—"

"Wait, I just figured it out. Tulip was his girl because

he was crazy about her and enjoyed having a warm physical relationship with her, but Cherry was more experimental about nutrition. So he kept bringing health food to Tulip and what the fish didn't eat Cherry ate. So he killed Cherry for the same reason he killed the fish. All in the interest of getting Tulip to stop eating cooked meat and other poisonous things. What's the matter? I think it's neat the way I tied it all together. Why don't you call Gregorio and tell him to pick up Henderson? I won't let on that it was all my idea. When I write up the case I'll give you all the credit."

"Fetch Miss Wolinski," he said. "Perhaps she'd like a cocktail before dinner."

"Maybe some carrot juice," I suggested. "Alcohol's bad for the vital bodily fluids."

He gave me a look and I went upstairs to fetch Tulip.

I don't know exactly what dinner consisted of but I'm sure Haskell Henderson would have turned green at the thought of it. Wong had marinated squares of beef in something or other, then sprinkled them with toasted sesame seeds and mixed in some stir-fried vegetables, and the whole thing came together beautifully as always. During the meal Haig talked with Tulip about the problems of breeding the *Ctenapoma* species. I didn't get the hang of more than a third of their conversation, and I won't plague you with any of it.

Afterward the three of us sat in the office. Tulip and I had coffee. So did Haig, who also had two Mounds bars in lieu of dessert. I picked up the phone and dialed Andrew Mallard's number again, and I got the same odd busy signal as before.

"Sometimes he just leaves it off the hook for long stretches of time," Tulip said. "He gets into these depressed states where he decides that there's no one on earth he could possibly want to talk to. It was really aggravating when I was living with him. I'd get calls for jobs and I would never know about it."

"What does he do if somebody rings his doorbell when he's in a state like that?"

"He generally answers it. But not always."

"That's great."

Haig said, "Miss Wolinski, you formerly shared that apartment. Do you still possess a key?"

"I think so. Yes, I'm sure I do. I think it's still on my key ring." She fumbled in her purse and detached a key from the ring. "This is it," she said.

"Might he have changed the locks? You moved out some time ago, I believe."

"It was five months ago." She thought for a moment. "No, he wouldn't change the locks. He'd think of it but he would never get around to it."

I wondered why she had ever set up housekeeping

with Mallard in the first place. He wasn't all that much to look at, and the more I heard about him the less enthusiastic I got about seeing him.

"You had better take that key," Haig said. "You needn't see Miss Remo or Miss Cubbage until late tonight. Mrs. Henderson can keep until tomorrow. Miss Tattersall can probably keep throughout eternity as far as we are concerned. A cranky old woman might be capable of harassment. Such persons frequently poison other people's dogs and cats. It's a form of paranoia, I believe. I cannot imagine her flipping curare-tipped darts at a topless dancer."

"She wouldn't even walk into Treasure Chest," Tulip said. "Not a chance."

I felt like a character in a comic strip with a little light bulb forming over my head. "Just a minute," I said. "Earlier today you said the person who poisoned the fish was someone different from the person who poisoned Cherry." Tulip gaped and started to say something but I pressed on. "Does that mean the Tattersall woman poisoned the fish? And how do you know that, and why don't I talk to her and find out why? Because we already decided the two things tied in, they had to tie in, and—"

Haig showed me the palm of his right hand. "Stop," he said. "Helen Tattersall did not poison the fish. Let us for the moment forget Helen Tattertsall entirely."

"Then who did poison the fish? And how—"

"In due course," Haig said. "There is a distinction between a surmise and conclusion. There is no need to air one's surmises. It's odd that Mr. Flatt hasn't called. When did you see him last, Miss Wolinski?"

She thought it over, trying to frown her memory into supplying the answer, and the phone picked that minute to ring. I reached for it but Haig waved me off and snatched it himself.

He said, "Hello? Ah, Mr. Flatt. I was expecting your call. Yes. Let me make this short and to the point. I am representing your ex-wife, Miss Thelma Wolinski, in an investigation of the murder of her roommate. . . . If you'll permit me to continue, Mr. Flatt. Thank you. I have only one question to ask you. Why did you quit the premises of Treasure Chest so abruptly last night when Miss Bounce was murdered? No, sir, the identification was positive. No, I have not informed them. The police and I do not pool our information, sir. Indeed." There was a pause, and Tulip and I spent it looking at each other. "I want you in my office tomorrow afternoon, Mr. Flatt. At three o'clock. No, make that three-thirty. I don't care what you tell your employers. Three-thirty. 311 1/2 West 20th Street, third floor. I look forward to it."

He hung up the phone and tried not to look smug. It was a nice try but he didn't quite make it.

Tulip said, "How did you know he was there? I didn't see him. Who told you?"

"Mr. Flatt told me. Just now."

"But you said—"

He shrugged. "Chip left a message for Mr. Flatt almost five hours ago. He might have called back immediately, routinely returning a call. He did not. He took time to establish that I am a detective and to stew a bit in his own juices. Then, knowing that I am a detective and guessing what I wanted of him, he ultimately returned my call. If he had called back immediately or not at all he might well have had nothing to hide. By taking the middle course, so to speak, he established to my satisfaction that he was at Treasure Chest last night."

This absolutely impressed the daylights out of Tulip. She couldn't get over how brilliant he was, and he was so delighted with her admiration that he celebrated with a Clark bar and rang Wong for more coffee.

Wong brought two cups. He must have sensed that I wasn't having any. I would have liked another cup but I would have had to stay in that room to drink it and that was out of the question. And he'd had the nerve to say phooey to my theory about Haskell Henderson and the health food conspiracy! I'd been babbling, for Pete's sake, but I'd come as close to reality as that load of crap about he-didn't-call-early-and-he-didn't-not-call.

It had been a bluff, pure and simple. If Flatt just told him he was crazy he could roll with the punch, and if Flatt bought the whole pitch then he was home free. It was a bluff, and a fairly standard bluff, and not too far removed from what I'd pulled on Henderson. I had to give him credit, he'd read his lines beautifully, but all it was was a bluff and the explanation he thought up later was just that, something he thought up afterward to fit the facts and make him look like the genius he wanted to be.

Of all the goddamned cheap grandstand plays, and of course Tulip bought it all across the board. And I'd had to sit there and watch. Well, I didn't have to put up with any more of it. I dialed Mallard's number once more, just as a matter of form, and then I scooped the key off the desk and got away from Miss Willing and Mr. Wonderful.

Andrew Mallard's apartment—by virtue of squatter's rights it was his, anyway—was on Arbor Street near the corner of Bank. I had more time than I needed to get his story before I was due at Treasure Chest, and I wanted to walk off some of the irritation I felt toward Haig, so I hiked down Eighth until it turned into Hudson Street, and then I groped around until I found Bank, made a lucky guess, and located Arbor Street. I usually get lost in the West Village, and the farther west I go the loster I get. I can find almost any place, but only if I start out in the right place. (I'm not the only one who has that trouble. When you've got a geometrically sensible city with streets running east and west and avenues running north and south, and then you rig up a neighborhood in which everything goes in curves and diagonals and Fourth Street intersects with Eleventh Street, you're just begging for trouble.)

I looked for a bell with Mallard on it and couldn't find one. Then I went through the listings carefully and found one that said Wolinski. He really was an inert type, no question about it. I mean, he'd been there five months by himself, and for a certain amount of time before that he'd shared the place with her, and her name was still on the bell and his wasn't.

I rang his bell and nothing happened. I rang it again and some more nothing happened, and I tried Tulip's key in the downstairs door and of course it didn't fit, it was the key to the apartment. I wondered why she hadn't given me both keys and then I wondered why this hadn't occurred to me earlier. I said a twelve-letter word that I don't usually say aloud, and then I rang a couple of other bells, and somebody pushed a buzzer and I opened the door.

Mallard's apartment was on the third floor. I knocked on his door for a while and nothing happened. I decided he was either out or asleep or catatonic and there was no point in persisting, but it had been a long walk and I had the damned key in my hand so I persisted.

At 8:37 I let myself into his apartment.

Ten

AT 8:51 I let myself out.

Eleven

I WALKED INTO the first bar I saw, went straight up to the bar and ordered a double Irish whiskey. The bartender poured it and I drank it right down. Then I paid for it, and I scooped up a dime from my change and headed for the phone booth in the rear. I invested the dime and dialed seven numbers and Leo Haig answered on the fourth ring.

I said, "How clean is our phone? Do you suppose we're all alone or do we have company?"

"Let us act as though we have company."

"Probably a good idea. I'm at a pay phone and I understand they're all tapped. But who has the time to monitor all of them? Of course if somebody was listening in I'd be a dead duck and that would make two tonight."

"I see."

"I was hoping you would."

"You're certain of the fact?"

"Positive."

"Do you know how the condition was induced?"

I shook my head, then realized that wouldn't work over the telephone. "No," I said. "He could have done it himself, he could have had help, or it might be God's will. No way I could tell."

"Hmmmm." I waited, and turned to glance through the fly-specked glass door of the phone booth. Several heads were turned in my direction. I turned away from them and Haig said, "I trust you have covered your traces."

"No. I took my lipstick and wrote *Catch me before I kill more* on the bathroom mirror."

"There is no need for sarcasm."

"I'm sorry," I said. "It shook me, I'll admit it. Do I report this?"

"Yes, and right away. Use a different phone."

"I know that."

"You said you were shaken."

"Not *that* shaken," I said. "Hell."

"Report the discovery and return here directly."

"Is our friend still with you? Because she's—"

"Yes," he cut in. "Don't waste time." And he hung up on me, which was probably all to the good because I really *was* a little rattled and I might have found ways to prolong the conversation indefinitely.

I went back to the bar and ordered another shot, a single this time, and a man came over to me and said, "Oh, let me buy you this one, why don't you. You seem terribly agitated. Nothing too alarming, I hope?"

I looked at him, and at some of the other customers, and I realized I was in a gay bar. "Oh," I said.

"I beg your pardon?"

I couldn't really resent it. You go drinking in a gay bar and people have the right to jump to conclusions. "Never mind," I said. "I don't want the drink anyway." I pocketed my change and left, feeling very foolish.

Two blocks over I found a booth on the street. I dialed 911 and changed my voice and told whoever it was that answered that there was a dead man at 134 Arbor Street and gave the apartment number and hung up before any questions could be asked of me. I walked another block and got in a cab.

I had found Andrew Mallard in the bedroom. The whole apartment had reeked of whiskey and vomit, and I figured he'd passed out. He was lying on his bed with his shoes off but the rest of his clothes on, laying on his back, a trickle of puke running from the corner of his mouth down his cheek.

I very nearly turned around and left at that point, and if I'd done that I'd have been in trouble, because I wouldn't have bothered wiping my fingerprints off the doorknob and a few other surfaces I'd touched. But something made me put my hand to his forehead. Maybe I sensed unconsciously that he wasn't breathing. Maybe I was toying with the idea of shaking him awake, though why would I have wanted a wide-awake drunk on my hands? For whatever reason, I did touch him, and he was cold, the kind of cold that you're not if you're alive. Then I reached for his hand and it was also cold, and his fingers were stiff, and at that point there was no getting around the fact that Andrew Mallard was a dead duck.

"But I can't tell you what killed him," I told Haig. "I counted five empty scotch bottles around the apartment, and that was without a particularly intensive search. If he emptied them all since the police let him go this morning then I know what killed him. Alcohol poisoning."

"He tended to leave garbage around," Tulip said. "I went back once for some stuff and there were newspapers three weeks old, and lots of empty bottles."

"Well, he emptied one of them today. The whole place smelled of booze and he reeked of it. I don't know if he drank enough to kill him."

Haig frowned. "You said he had been sick."

"You mean he threw up? Yes. Not a lot, though. Just a trickle."

"Hmmmm."

"He could have been poisoned. He could have had a

heart attack or a stroke. I couldn't tell anything from what I saw, but then I'm not a medical examiner, I don't know what to look for. If his throat had been cut or if there was a bullet hole in his head I probably would have noticed. Then again, somebody could have strangled him or shot him in the chest and I probably *wouldn't* have noticed. I didn't want to disturb the body or anything."

"That was wise," Haig said. "The police will determine cause of death and time of death. They are sound enough in that area. Any efforts you might have made would only have served to render their work more difficult."

"That's what I figured."

"Did anyone see you enter the building?"

"I don't know. I wasn't trying to avoid being seen. I made sure nobody saw me leave. Anyway it doesn't really matter if they can prove I was there around 8:30. I don't know how long he was dead, I don't know how long it takes a body to lose body heat, but it was awhile."

Haig nodded absently, then leaned back in his chair. This time he kept his feet on the floor. His hand went to his beard and petted it affectionately.

I turned to Tulip. The expression on her face was like the one I had seen last night when Cherry was killed, a sort of numb look.

"It's so hard to believe," she said. "I slept with him,

I lived with him. I was in love with him." She stopped to consider, then amended this. "At least I *thought* I was in love with him. For a while. And then he got to be a kind of a habit, you know. He was there and he needed me, and it took awhile to break the habit. But it's horrible that he's dead. He was a very nice man. He was a loser, you know, but he was a decent sort of a guy. If he could ever have gotten ahold of himself he would have been all right, but he never quite managed to, and now he never will, will he?"

I moved my chair away from the desk and closer to hers. She reached out a hand and I took it. Her hands were large—everything about her was large, for Pete's sake—but her fingers were very long and thin, and the touch of her hand was cool. She got her hand around mine and squeezed. There was a sad half-smile on her face and her eyes looked to be backed up with tears she had no intention of shedding.

"We shall have to play something of a waiting game," Haig said thoughtfully. "Three possibilities exist. No, four. Mallard could have been murdered. He could have committed suicide. He could have had a heart attack or something of the sort. Finally, he could have committed a sort of involuntary suicide due to overindulgence in alcohol. I don't suppose there was an empty bottle of sleeping tablets beside the bed?"

"It's the sort of thing I probably would have mentioned."

"Quite." Haig heaved a sigh. I'd say he heaved it just about halfway across the room. "We'll act on the supposition that the man was murdered. All deaths in the course of a homicide investigation ought to be regarded as homicides themselves until proven otherwise. It's by far the best working hypothesis. Miss Wolinski."

"Yes?"

"You will remain here this evening. There is a reasonably comfortable bed in the guest room. Wong Fat will change the linen for you. There is a murderer on the loose and he has already demonstrated that he can gain access to your apartment. I would be remiss in my duties if I permitted you to spend the night alone. I will brook no argument."

"I wasn't going to argue," Tulip said.

"Oh? Then you are a rational woman, and I am delighted. Mr. Harrison always resists my urgings to spend the night. But he too will stay here."

"No argument," I said.

"Oh? Extraordinary."

I didn't see what was so extraordinary about it. Anybody who wouldn't welcome the chance to spend the night under the same roof as Tulip needed hormone shots.

"Wong will make up the couch for you," he went on. "But first you have some places to go and some people to see."

*   *   *

Buddy Lippa was wearing a sport jacket that would have kept him safe in the hunting season. It had inch-square checks of bright orange and black, and I had the feeling that it glowed in the dark. He was also wearing blue-and-white striped slacks, a canary silk shirt, and a troubled frown. "You're gettin' to be a regular," he said. "I don't know if it's such a good idea. Bein' as you're underage and all."

"I showed proof of age last night," I reminded him. "I can't afford another ten."

"Oh, I wasn't lookin' for that. All it is, the boss might get tired of seein' you. Say, you happen to know when Tulip's gonna be workin' again? The two bimbos we got on tonight are strictly from Doggie Heaven."

I told him Tulip wasn't sure when she'd be returning to work. He let me through and I went up to the bar and ordered a bottle of beer. Jan uncapped it and poured it into a glass for me. "How's Tulip?" she wanted to know. "Is it true she was arrested? Are you really a detective? Do they know who murdered Cherry?"

I said, "She's fine. Yes, I am. No, they don't, but Leo Haig is working on it."

She squinted for a moment and assigned the three answers to the three questions. She started to say something else but some clown from Iowa was tapping his glass impatiently on the bar to indicate that it was empty. She moved off to take care of him. I looked up at the stage and watched a rather skinny blonde move around. She had a vacant expression on her face and whatever music she was dancing to was not the music they were playing. I guessed that she was tripping on something, either mescaline or speed. Whichever it was she probably did a lot of it, which would help to explain why she looked like she was suffering from terminal starvation. Her ribcage was more prominent than her breasts.

"Jesus, you again." I turned around and it was Gus Leemy and he still looked like a bald penguin, except now he looked like a constipated bald penguin. "Finish the beer and move on," he said. "Guys like you could cost me my license. No hard feelings, but I want to stay in business." He accompanied this last sentence with the most unconvincing smile anyone has ever flashed at me.

"I could cost you your license anyway," I said. "How long do you think you'd stay open if Leo Haig decided to go after you? There's a racket going on in your own club and you don't even know about it. You should be more worried about that than about me drinking a beer."

His eyes widened. "I don't know what you're talking about," he said.

"Of course you don't. That's the whole point. I think you'd better show up at Leo Haig's office tomorrow at three-thirty in the afternoon."

"What's it all about?"

"Three-thirty tomorrow," I said. "That's when you'll find out."

He started to say something else but changed his mind. He gave me a long look. I held his eyes for a few seconds, then turned back to my beer. If he'd kept up a barrage of questions I don't know exactly where I would have gone with them. It's easy to say *no comment* to a reporter, but reporters don't have Buddy Lippa around to hit you if you give them a hard time. I think this may have been running through his mind. Anyway, he decided against it and left me to drink my beer in peace.

I moved down the bar to where the waitresses came to pick up their drinks. I sat there nursing my beer. Maeve O'Connor came over after a few minutes to order three whiskey sours and a pousse-café. Jan said she didn't know how to make a pousse-café and it was no time for her to experiment. Maeve said she'd see what else they'd settle for and went away. She hadn't noticed me, which was sad. She came back and said to change the pousse-café to a stinger, and I said hello, and she smiled as if genuinely pleased to see me. Which was nice.

I asked if her boss was around. She said he'd dropped in earlier but had left about an hour and a half ago.

"The other waitress," I said. "Is that Rita Cubbage?

The girl who was working last night?" Maeve nodded.
"I'd like to talk with her," I said. "Ask her to stop by
for a minute."

Rita Cubbage turned out to be a black girl wearing a
blond wig. I hoped she took it off when she left the
club; most of the Times Square hookers wear wigs like
that, and if Rita walked down the street with it on she
probably got a lot of offers.

I said, "Hello. My name's Chip Harrison and I work
for Leo Haig."

"The detective," she said. "Maeve told me. You
were here last night, weren't you?"

"Yes, but were you? Not with that wig."

"No, I left it off last night. Do you like it?"

"It's striking," I said.

"You don't like it." She grinned. "That's all right.
Neither do I. But it boosts the tips, if you can dig it. My
hair's normally in an Afro and it puts the dudes uptight because they figure I must be terribly militant.
This way they figure I put out."

I asked her about what she had seen last night, and
what she knew about Cherry and Tulip and the other
people involved in the case. She didn't seem to know
very much. There wasn't much point to it, as far as I
could see, but I invited her to come to Haig's house at
three-thirty. If he wanted a party, the least I could do
was provide a full list of guests. She copied down the
street address and put the tip of the pencil between
her lips, a sudden frown of concentration on her face.

"Something," she said.

"You can't make it?"

"Oh, I guess I can. Something just on the tip of my tongue and now I can't get hold of it. You know how that'll happen?"

"Something about last night?"

"No, goes back a few days. Damn."

"Maybe it'll come to you."

"I just know it will," she said. "What I'll do, I'll sleep on it. Then in the middle of the night it'll come to me."

"Keep paper and pencil on the table next to your bed so you can write it down."

"Oh, that's what I always do. I'll be sleeping, and all of a sudden something'll pop into my head, and I'll write it down. Only thing is half the time the next morning I won't know what it means. Like one time I woke up and there was the pad of paper on the bedside table, and what it said on it was, 'Every silver lining has a cloud.' "

"That's really far out."

"Yeah, but what did I have in mind? Never did figure that one out." She winked. "See you tomorrow, Chip."

I went back to my beer. When Maeve came to pick up an order of drinks I gave her the same invitation. "And tell your boss it would be a good idea for him to show up, too. Three-thirty at Haig's place."

A few minutes later I got to extend the invitation to Jan Remo. I waited until she was pouring me a second beer and then I told her the time and place. If her hand shook any, I didn't notice it.

"Three-thirty," she said. "I suppose I can make it. I'm having my hair done earlier but I should be through in plenty of time. But what's it all about?"

"Mr. Haig doesn't tell me everything," I said. "If I had to guess, I'd say he intends to trap a murderer."

"I thought the police solve murders."

"They do, occasionally. So does Leo Haig."

"And you're his assistant."

"That's right."

"Does Mr. Haig know who killed Cherry?"

"I told you he doesn't tell me everything. That's one of the things he hasn't told me."

She broke off the conversation to fill a drink order, then got Maeve's attention and asked her to handle the bar while she took a break. "You won't have to do much," she said. "If you don't push drinks at them they don't order much. Just cover for me while I go to the head."

I chatted with Maeve for a few minutes. Not about murder or other nasty things but about her career in show business and how she had a driving need to make a success of herself. I was pleased to hear this. It's a theory of mine that women with one driving need have other driving needs as well, which tends to make them more interesting company than other women. I don't know how valid this is, but I guess it'll do until a better theory comes along.

We didn't have all that much time to talk before Jan was back. They stood side by side for a moment, both of them rather spectacular to look at and both of them redheads, and a part of my mind started thinking idly in troilistic terms, which I gather is a fairly standard male fantasy. I suppose it's something I'll have to try sooner or later, but I have the feeling it wouldn't be as terrific in actuality as it is in fantasy, because it would be hard to concentrate and you wouldn't know which way to turn. At any rate, I was fairly certain I wouldn't get to try it with Maeve and Jan. I had the feeling they were less than crazy about one another.

Then Maeve went back to her tables and Jan said, "I guess I'll be there tomorrow, Chip. But there's really nothing I know. Nothing that would help."

"You were right here when she got killed," I said. "Didn't you see anything at all?"

"The police asked me all that."

"Well, maybe you saw something and didn't know you saw it. I mean, you know, it didn't seem important at the time."

"I didn't even see it," she said. "I was pouring a drink. The first I knew something was wrong was when everybody took a deep breath all at once. Then I turned around and Cherry was lying on the stage and that was the first I saw of it."

"Well, I think you should come tomorrow anyway."

"I will."

I finished most of my beer and decided I could live without the rest of it. I left some change on the bar for Jan, decided it was a puny tip and added a dollar bill. I nodded a sort of collective goodnight on the chance that someone was looking my way and I walked to the door and out onto Seventh Avenue.

I thought about a cab and decided I would take the subway instead. The AA train stops at Eighth Avenue and Fiftieth, so I started uptown, and I walked about ten steps and felt a pair of hands take hold of my right arm. I was just getting ready to find out who owned them when two more hands took hold of my left arm and a voice said, "Easy does it, kid."

I said, "Oh, come on. It's the middle of Times Square and there are cops all over the place."

"Oh, yeah? I don't see no cops around, kid. Where are all the cops?"

Collecting graft, I decided. Sleeping in their cars. Because I couldn't see a single cop anywhere. I heard a calypso verse once that maintained that policemen, women, and taxi cabs are never there when you want them. It's the God's honest truth.

"We're just gonna take a nice ride," the voice said. They were walking me along and they had my arms in a disturbingly effective grip.

"Suppose I don't want to go?"

"That would be silly."

"Getting in a car would be sillier."

"Now what you got to do is use your head," said another voice, the one on my left. "A man wants to talk to you. That's all there is to it. He says not to hurt you long as you cooperate. What the hell, you're cooperating, aren't you? There's the car, right around the corner, and you're walking to it like a nice reasonable kid. So what's the problem?"

"Who's the boss?"

"The guy we're going to see."

"Yeah, right," I said. We walked up to the car, a long low Lincoln with a black man behind the wheel. He was wearing sunglasses, his head was shaved, there was a gold earring in his ear, and he had a little gold spoon on a gold chain around his neck. That's either a sign that you use cocaine or that you want people to think you do.

I said, "Look, tell me who the boss is or I don't get in the car."

"If we want you to get in the car, kid, there's not a hell of a lot you can do about it."

"I can make it easier," I said. "Just tell me who we're going to see."

One of them let go of my arms and stepped around to where I could see him. He wasn't much to look at, but he didn't have to be to do his job. He looked like a hood, which stood to reason, because that was evidently what he was.

He said, "What the hell, you'll know in ten minutes anyway. The boss is Mr. Danzig. You gonna get in the car now?"

"Oh, sure," I said. "I mean, why not? I was supposed to see him anyway."

Twelve

I DON'T KNOW what I expected exactly. He had already surprised me. I'd had the impression that he was very small-time, not important enough to have a couple of musclemen and a driver working for him. Of course he could have hired them for the occasion from Hertz Rent-a-Hood, but somehow I doubted this.

But whatever I had expected, he wasn't it. He was waiting for me in a penthouse apartment on top of a high-rise on York Avenue in the Eighties. One whole wall of the living room was glass, and you could look out across the East River and gaze at more of the Borough of Queens than anyone in his right mind would want to see. He was doing just that when we walked in, all dolled up in a black mohair suit and holding a glass of something-on-the-rocks in his hand. When he turned to look at me I got the feeling he was disappointed that it was only me and not the photographer from *Playgirl* magazine.

But he wasn't disappointed at all. He flashed me a smile that showed almost as many teeth as Haskell Henderson's without looking half as phony. "You must be Mr. Harrison," he said. "I'm so glad to see you."

He crossed the room. This wasn't as easy as it sounds because there was a lot of room to cross and all of it was covered by a light blue carpet deep enough to make walking a tricky proposition. He transferred his drink to his left hand and held out his right hand. I took it, and we shook hands briskly, and he let me have the smile again.

"I hope these gentlemen behaved properly," he said, indicating the two muscle types. The driver had stayed with the car. "And let me apologize for the manner in which I had you brought here. In my field, the direct approach is often the only possible approach. You weren't abused, I hope?"

"No."

"That's good to know," he said. He smiled past me at the two heavies. "That's all for tonight," he said. "And thanks very much."

There was something about the way he talked that made his sentences go on ringing in my head after he was done saying them. You just knew that he hadn't talked like this years ago, and that he wouldn't speak the same words or use the same accent if, say, you woke him up suddenly in the middle of the night. He was all dressed up in a suit as good as one of Gregorio's, and he had at least as good a barber, and his teeth were capped by the world's greatest dentist, and underneath it all you had a hard tough monkey who could beat a man to death with a baseball bat and then go home and tuck himself in for a good eight hours' sleep.

I had met the type before. Haig has a good friend named John LiCastro who spends a lot of his time sipping espresso in a neighborhood social club on Mulberry Street, making little executive decisions, such as who lives and who dies. LiCastro raises tropical fish, mostly cichlids, and when his fish die he practically puts on a black arm band. Leonard Danzig was an up-to-date version of the same type.

"You'll want something to drink," he said to me now. "I believe you generally drink beer. I have Heineken's and Lowenbrau."

There's nothing wrong with either, but I'd had enough beer. I asked if he happened to have Irish whiskey. He didn't, and he seemed genuinely apologetic. He gave me my choice of three different brands of expensive scotch. I took Dewar's Ancestor, which turned out to be what he was drinking, too. He made a drink for me and freshened his own and motioned me to a pair of chairs near the wall of glass. He took one and I took the other and we both sipped whiskey.

He said, "I have a problem. It started last night

when Cherry was murdered. It's not getting simpler. It's getting more difficult."

I didn't say anything.

"You're with Leo Haig. He's a private detective. I also understand he's something of an oddball."

I admitted that some people probably thought so. I didn't bother to add that I was one of them.

"But I also understand he gets results."

"Well, he's a genius," I said. "And the only way to prove he's a genius is by solving impossible crimes, so that's what he does. He gets results."

"So I've heard." Danzig leaned forward, set his glass down on top of a small marble-topped table. He didn't use a coaster. Either glasses don't leave rings on marble or he didn't care. He could always throw the table away. I kept my drink in my hand. He said, "Cherry was a friend of mine, you know."

"I know."

"I had been seeing her for about a month, maybe a little longer than that. I probably would have gone on seeing her for another month. No more than that." He smiled disarmingly. "I don't seem to be very good at sticking to a woman. I find that any reasonably good-looking woman can be exciting company for perhaps two months. Then they become boring."

I didn't have an answer for that one.

"Unfortunately," he went on, "Cherry was murdered. I'm sorry about that if only because I genuinely liked her. She was a warm, sweet person." The smile went away. "I'm particularly sorry that she happened to be killed while I was involved with her. It's awkward for me. As long as the case remains unsolved, the police have an excuse to intrude in my affairs. They might even keep the case open on purpose in order to provide themselves with an excuse to harass me. In my business, that's a liability."

I didn't ask him what his business was.

"It's unfortunate that I have to be exposed to this simply because of my friendship for Cherry. I've been friendly with quite a few of the young ladies who've worked at Treasure Chest. I go there frequently, I get acquainted with the people who work there. The dancers, the barmaids, the waitresses. I'm in a position to be of assistance to them in their careers, you understand. And they like a taste of the high life. They work hard, they don't earn all that much money, they appreciate a decent dinner and civilized company."

"I see," I said. I didn't, if you want to know, but it was something to say.

"You familiar with a fellow named Andrew Mallard?"

"I never met him."

"Neither did I," Danzig said. He smiled again. "That's not what I asked."

"I know who he is." (I'm very proud of that sentence, let me tell you. Is. Not was. That's thinking on your feet, if I say so myself.)

"Was," Danzig said. "Not is. He died tonight."

"Oh?" (I'm less proud of that sentence, but they can't all be zingers.)

He nodded. "It was just on the radio. They identified him as a former close associate of Tulip Willing, roommate of murdered dancer Cherry Bounce. Somebody tipped the police and they found him dead in bed. His bed."

"How did he die?"

"Choked to death on his own vomit," Danzig said. He picked up his scotch and took a dainty sip. "Got drunk, passed out, then threw up in his sleep and sucked it into his lungs or something. You all right?"

"Just a little nauseous."

"Yeah, well, it's only dangerous if you happen to be unconscious at the time. Freshen that drink for you?"

"No thanks."

He crossed to the bar and put another ounce or so of scotch in his own glass. "Now here's my line of thought," he went on, returning to his chair. "I think it would be very convenient if it happened to turn out that Andrew Mallard murdered Cherry. He was there. He could have done it. Any list of suspects would have to have him on it, wouldn't you say?"

"I suppose so."

"There it is," he said. "All Leo Haig has to do is prove Mallard killed Cherry. Then he got full of remorse over what he'd done and did some heavy drinking. And so on. How do you like it?"

"Well, it's certainly possible."

"That's the ticket." He drew an alligator wallet from his jacket pocket and pulled out a sheaf of bills. They were hundreds, and he counted out ten of them, paused, studied me for a moment, and counted out ten more. I don't know what he saw in my face that doubled the ante. Maybe the whole thing was just theatrics. "Two thousand dollars," he said.

"Uh."

Then he did something incredible. He took the twenty bills and tore them in half. I guess I wasn't perfect at keeping a straight face, because he grinned at my expression.

"For Haig," he said, offering me what managed to be half of two thousand dollars without being one thousand dollars. "Here, take it. He gets the other half when he proves that Andrew Mallard murdered Cherry Bounce. That's if he brings it off within three days. Take it."

I took it because it was impossible not to, but instead of holding onto it I set it down on the table next to Leonard Danzig's glass of scotch. "There's one problem," I said.

"Let's hear it. I'm usually fairly good at straightening out problems."

I could believe it. I said, "The thing is, you don't know Mr. Haig. I'm not saying he wouldn't work for you, but suppose Andrew Mallard didn't murder Cherry Bounce? Suppose someone else did?"

Danzig thought this over. I'd hate to play poker

with him. Nothing at all showed in his face. At length he shrugged and said, "All right, I just thought it was easier that way. No loose ends. What I'm concerned with is the time element. If Haig gets the murderer in three days he gets the other half of the two thousand. How's that?"

"Whoever the murderer is?"

"Whoever."

I asked if I could use the phone. He pointed at one halfway across the room. I don't suppose it was more than forty yards from me. "It might be tapped," he said. "I pay a guy to check them out periodically, but he hasn't been around for a few days."

I told him it didn't matter. I didn't dial Haig's number because the phone had buttons instead of a dial. I *pushed* Haig's number and got him. I said, "I'm at Mr. Leonard Danzig's apartment. I just learned that Andrew Mallard died earlier today. It was on the radio." I went on to tell him the cause of death, then brought him up to date on Danzig's proposal and my counter-proposal. He said "Satisfactory" a couple of times, which made me very proud of myself, and then he talked some more and I listened. Finally he said, "I am going to sleep now, Chip. Don't disturb me when you return. Your report can wait until morning. You made all the necessary arrangements?"

"Yes."

"Goodnight, then. And come directly home when you leave Mr. Danzig's apartment."

I said I would and hung up. To Danzig I said, "Mr. Haig says I should take your money."

Danzig smiled and pointed to the little pile of bills.

"There are a couple of qualifiers first. You mentioned a three-day limit."

"If it went a few hours over—"

"That's not the point. Would it be worth a bonus if Haig wrapped it up within twenty-four hours. Say tomorrow afternoon?"

"It wouldn't hurt any. What kind of a bonus?"

I was supposed to use my judgment on this one, so I judged quickly. "Double," I said. "Four thousand if it's wrapped up tomorrow. Two thousand if we make the three-day limit. Beyond that you don't owe us anything and you get the stack of homemade fifties back."

"Done."

"All right. The second point is that I'm supposed to ask you some questions now. Mr. Haig said he's assuming that you did not kill Cherry and don't know who did. He says only a rank fool would hire him under those circumstances, and I've used my intelligence guided by my experience to decide that you're not a fool."

"I'm honored."

"Were you at Treasure Chest the night Cherry was murdered?"

"Yes."

The admission was so direct that it stopped me

momentarily. I got back into gear and said, "Were you there when it happened?"

"I was on the premises."

"You missed the police dragnet."

"I went out the back. I didn't know it was murder but I gathered she was dead and I didn't want to be found on the premises in an official investigation."

"Are you the owner of Treasure Chest?"

"Let's say I'm a good friend of Gus Leemy's. Will that do for the moment?"

"Sure. Do you have any idea who might want to kill Cherry?"

"No one now. She's already dead."

"I mean—"

He crossed one leg over the other. "Just a small joke," he said. "No, frankly, I have no suspects. I rather like the idea of Andrew Mallard, but that's simply because it would be so convenient that way. And he seemed to be a disturbed person. Would a sane man choose that way to kill a woman?"

I wanted to say that a sane man wouldn't kill anybody for any reason but I didn't know how well this would go down, because I had the feeling that Danzig had killed people now and then, or had had them killed, and this would mean calling him a lunatic by implication.

"And you saw nothing suspicious?"

"Nothing. I was in no position to see anything at the

time the incident occurred. I was in the office in the rear with Gus."

"Was anyone else with you at the time? I don't mean that you and Gus can't alibi each other, that's all right. But if other people were with you we could also rule them out."

"I'm afraid we were alone together."

I drank the last of my scotch. It was really great scotch. I said I guessed that was about it. "Mr. Haig wants you at his office at three-thirty tomorrow afternoon," I said. "You might as well bring the other half of the two thousand. Plus another two thousand."

He got to his feet and we began the long walk to the door. "Three-thirty," he said. "I'll be there. I wouldn't want to miss it. He really thinks he can come through in that short a time?"

"Evidently. He wants to earn the bonus."

But the bonus wasn't the big consideration, I knew. What Haig really wanted was the applause.

Thirteen

THE CAB DROPPED me at West 20th Street around two-thirty. I used one key to let myself into the courtyard, climbed two flights of stairs, and used another key to let me into Haig's half of the house. There was a light on in the office and I guessed that he hadn't been to sleep after all, but when I went in ready to hit him with some smartass remark or other his chair was empty and Tulip was sitting on the couch reading a Fredric Brown novel. *Mrs. Murphy's Underpants*, one of the late ones.

"This is pretty good," she said. "Have you read it?"

"Sure. Mr. Haig made me read everything of Fredric Brown's. That's not supposed to be one of his best."

"I'm enjoying it anyway. I like the way the two detectives play against each other. An uncle and a nephew."

"Ed and Am Hunter, right."

"Do you and Mr. Haig interact the same way?"

"Not exactly. Of course we're not related, which helps. Or hinders. I'm never entirely sure which. Also Ambrose Hunter is supposed to be reasonably sane."

"Well, Mr. Haig—"

"Is crazy," I said.

"But—"

"That doesn't mean he isn't a genius. Maybe all geniuses are crazy. I couldn't honestly say. For instance, thirteen hours from now he's going to trap a murderer. Don't ask me how because I don't know. Don't ask him, either, because I'm not convined he knows, and even if he does he's not telling. But he's going to have the whole crowd here, all sitting on chairs with their hands folded, and if he doesn't deliver he's going to look like Babe Ruth would have looked if he pointed to the fence and then struck out. The one thing he doesn't want is to look ridiculous, and with his shape and mannerisms he has a good head start in that direction, so he really has to deliver. And he probably will, but don't ask me how."

"It's kind of exciting," she said.

I agreed that it was. I said I thought I'd have a beer and asked her if she wanted anything. She didn't. I uncapped the beer in the kitchen and brought the bottle into the office with me. I asked her when Haig had gone to sleep.

"Right after he got your call. He said he was very tired. I guess he didn't get much sleep last night."

"Nobody did," I said, and yawned. "I'm completely shot myself. As soon as I finish this beer and unwind a little I'm going to stretch out on the couch and make Z's."

"Oh! I'm sorry, this is where you're going to be sleeping, isn't it? I'll go upstairs now."

I waved her back to the couch. "I have to unwind first," I said. "And you're the one who ought to be exhausted. Did you get any sleep last night?"

"Not really. They kept moving me around from one stationhouse to another."

"Yeah, the old cop shuffle. The hell of it is that they knew damned well you didn't kill Cherry. They just wanted to give you a hard time because you were Haig's client." I yawned. "Ed and Am Hunter. That's funny. Am Hunter was in a carnival for years. Can you see Leo Haig as a pitchman? I can't."

"Oh, I don't know." She considered, then giggled. I liked her wide-open laugh better.

"What's so funny?"

"Well, Ed Hunter certainly goes over well with the girls in this book."

"Thanks," I said.

"No, I meant it as a compliment."

"You did?"

"Well, yeah. You probably do pretty well yourself.

And the two of you do play off each other the same way, even if you're not related."

"We were almost related," I said. "A couple of months ago the cops picked me up and held me for seventy-two hours. They were just making a nuisance of themselves. As usual."

(It was an interesting case, incidentally. I never wrote it up because there wasn't enough to it to make a book out of it, and there was no sex in it, and Joe Elder at Gold Medal insists it's impossible to sell a book without sex in it. Maybe I'll try to write it up as a magazine story one of these days.)

Tulip frowned. "I don't get it," she said. "I mean, it's terrible that they locked you up and all, but how does that make you and Haig almost related?"

"It doesn't *make* us almost related. What it did was *almost* make us related. See, they wouldn't let him visit me in jail because he was neither a relative nor an attorney. He decided this might come up in the future so what he wanted to do was adopt me. He said it made perfect sense considering that my parents are dead. I told him it was ridiculous because I might someday become a partner in the firm."

"So?"

"So Haig & Harrison is possible," I said. "But Haig & Haig is ridiculous, unless you happen to be producing scotch whiskey. That wasn't the reason I wanted to avoid being adopted but it was a reason that made perfect sense to him, and—"

She began to laugh, and I joined in, and we really did quite a bit of hard-core laughing. Then we stopped as suddenly as we started and Tulip looked at me with her upper lip trembling slightly and I thought she was going to cry. I sat on the couch next to her and took hold of her hand.

"Everything's so funny," she said, "and then I remember that Cherry's dead and Andy's dead and I don't know how I can laugh at anything. And the murderer must be someone I know. That's the most frightening thing in the world. Somebody I know committed murder."

I put an arm around her and she sort of settled in against my shoulder. I gave her shoulder a squeeze and took her hand with my other hand.

"Who do you think did it, Chip?"

"I don't know."

"Could it have been Andy?"

"I suppose it could have been anybody. How did he get on with Cherry?"

"I'm not even sure they ever met. Where would he get hold of poison? Where would he get a key to my apartment? I don't understand."

"Neither do I."

"I'm just so confused."

She snuggled closer and I got a healthy lungful of her perfume. It was all I needed. I mean, the whole scene was beginning to get a little strange. I was playing a kind of comforting Big Brother role, which was weird in that she was not only older than me but bigger. And at the same time she was turning me on something terrible, and it shouldn't have been that way because the scene itself wasn't fundamentally sexual, but go tell yourself that when you're turned on. I looked down at her body and remembered what it looked like with no clothes on it, dancing merrily away on the stage at Treasure Chest, and then I closed my eyes because the sight of her was doing things to me, and having my eyes shut didn't really help at all because I could see her just as well with them shut.

"It's all so rotten," she said.

I took a breath. "Look," I said, "I think you'd better go to sleep, Tulip. It's late and you're exhausted, we're both exhausted. Things will look better in the morning."

"That's what people always say, isn't it?"

"Well, I didn't claim to originate the line."

"Maybe things *will* look better in the morning. But will they *be* any better?"

"Uh."

"I guess you're right," she said. She got to her feet. "Could you show me where my room is?"

I walked her to her room. "Come in for a minute," she said. "You don't mind, do you?"

We went into the room. She flicked on a light. The

bed had been opened and Wong had changed the sheets. I hadn't really had enough time to dirty them.

"It looks comfortable," she said.

"I'm not sure whether it is or not. I spent a couple hours on it this morning, but I was too tired to notice whether the bed was any good. It probably beats the couch. I slept on that one night before Haig bought the bed and it was like spending a night on the rack. I woke up with my spine in the shape of the letter S."

"Oh, and now you have to sleep on it again because of me! I'm sorry, Chip."

I used both hands to get my foot out of my mouth. It was a struggle. "Oh, I was exaggerating," I said, not too convincingly, I think. "It's not really all that bad. Anyway as tired as I am it won't make any difference." I made myself yawn. "See? Can't keep my eyes open. Well, goodnight, Tulip. Guess I'll see you in the morning, and in the meantime—"

"Chip?"

"What?"

"Look, we don't really know each other, and maybe this is silly, and of course I'm probably too old for you and you couldn't possibly be interested, but—"

"Tulip?"

"Don't go, Chip."

It started off being basically closeness and warmth and comfort, and we were both deliciously exhausted, and we drifted gradually into a beautiful lazy kind of lovemaking. Then it stopped being lazy and we stopped being aware that we were all that exhausted, and then we stopped being aware of much of anything, actually, and then, well, it became too good to talk about.

And a while later she said, "I thought it might turn you off. Me being older than you."

"Oh, sure. You really turned me off, Tulip. That's what you did, all right. Like a bucket of cold water."

She giggled. It was a pretty sexy giggle, actually. "Well, I thought it might turn *me* off, then. I was attracted to you, you know, but I'm used to older men. And we were both so tired but I wanted to do it anyway." She put her hand on my stomach and moved it gradually lower. "You must be really exhausted now," she said, holding on to me. "Oh."

"Uh-huh."

"How did you get so wide awake so fast?"

"It's one of the advantages of younger men," I said. "We have these incredible recuperative powers. Especially when we're in bed with somebody like you."

"How nice," she said. "But you must be tired."

"I'm not *that* tired," I said.

The last conscious thought I had was that I'd damn well better get from her bed to the couch before I fell asleep. Because Haig would either say something or maintain a diplomatic silence, and one would be as infuriating as the other. I had that thought, all right, but that was as far as it went. The next morning I knew it was morning.

Fourteen

I WAS THE last one awake. I yawned and stretched and reached for Tulip and encountered nothing but air and linen. I yawned some more and got up and put clothes on. They were having breakfast. I slipped out without saying hello, walked the few blocks to my own rooming house, showered and changed clothes and went back to Haig's. By then they were in the office and the great man was on the telephone. I couldn't tell who was on the other end of the line or what they were talking about, because all Haig said was "Yes" and "No" and "Indeed" and, at last, "Satisfactory." For all I could tell he had called the weather bureau and was talking back to the recording.

"There you are," he said to me. "I thought you'd gone off without instructions. You'll want to see Mrs. Henderson without further delay. And there are other errands for you as well."

I got out my notebook.

"I also want your report. Last night, from the time you left for Treasure Chest until your return. Verbatim, please."

I came as close to verbatim as possible and he listened to it with his feet on the desk. When I'd brought it to the point where I left Danzig at his apartment and hopped a cab home, he took his feet off the desk and leaned forward and frowned at me. "How did Mr. Danzig know where to find you?" he demanded.

"I thought about that. Jan Remo."

"The barmaid."

I nodded. "She excused herself to go to the bathroom. I don't think she went to the bathroom. I think she went to the telephone."

"And called Mr. Danzig."

"Right. I think she fingered me. That's the right term, isn't it?"

"I believe so."

"Well, I believe she fingered me." I pictured Jan, the red hair, the feline face, the fishnet stockings, the body stocking filled with just what I'd always wanted for Christmas. "She fingered me," I said. "I'd like to return the favor."

"I beg your pardon?"

"Just thinking out loud," I said.

Haig grunted—his way of thinking out loud—and spun around to consider the Rasboras. I looked over at

Tulip and she gave me the world's most solemn wink. I don't know if I blushed or not. I probably did.

Haig turned around again. "There's another variable. Rather surprising. You had a telephone call this morning during your absence."

"Oh?"

"From another topless dancer, I assume. One of those inane stage names." He turned to Tulip. "Your pardon, Miss Wolinski. No criticism is intended."

She assured him none was inferred.

"I don't recall that you've mentioned this one," he went on. "You know your reports must be as comprehensive as possible. The slightest detail—"

"There was no other dancer. Oh, there were a couple new ones last night, but I didn't talk to them. I didn't even get their names, and if that was an oversight I'm sorry. Who was it that called?"

He consulted a slip of paper. "She gave her name as Clover Swann," he said. "I've no idea what her real name might chance to be. She left a number."

"Oh, for Pete's sake," I said. "She's not a topless dancer."

"Indeed?"

"She's an editor," I said. "At Gold Medal." The image of Clover Swann, Gold Medal's resident hippie, dancing nude on the stage of Treasure Chest, suddenly flashed somewhere in my mind. It was by no means an unappealing image, but I had the feeling she was happier editing books.

"It was not an illogical assumption," Haig said. "Clover Swann indeed."

"Well, she's an editor. She probably wants to know when I'm going to do another book for them. I'll call her tomorrow or the next day."

"You'll call her now."

I just looked at him.

"Now," he repeated. "Bear in mind, Chip, that I hired you as much for your journalistic ability as anything else. It is not enough to be a brilliant detective. The world must know that one is a brilliant detective. Call Miss Swann. I have the number right here."

"I know the number," I said. I picked up the phone and dialed it, and after I'd given the operator everything but my Social Security number I got through to Clover.

"I've been reading the papers," she said. "It sounds as though you're right in the middle of an exciting case. Topless dancers and everything."

"And everything," I agreed.

"It ought to be perfect for your next book. Are you going to write it up?"

"That depends," I said. "A few hours from now Mr. Haig is going to reach into a hat. If he pulls out a rabbit I'll have something to write about. If he comes up empty it's not going to make much of a book."

Haig scribbled furiously, passed me a note. I read it quickly. It said: *"Show more enthusiasm."*

Clover must have read the note because she showed

plenty of enthusiasm. She went on telling me what a great book it would make, that it had all the ingredients. "And it should be a cinch to have a lot of sex in this one," she said. "You know what Joe always says."

I knew what he said, all right. *"People like to read about what a character Haig is and all that, Chip, but if you want to sell books to them you have to give them a hard-on."* That's what he always said.

"I'm not sure there's too much sex in it," I said.

"Oh, who do you think you're kidding?" She laughed heartily. "Topless dancers? Chip Harrison cavorting with a batch of topless dancers? If I know you, you're bouncing around like a satyr in a harem."

"Er," I said.

"Just let me know how it goes today, Chip, and we'll draw up a contract. You could even start thinking about a title."

"Uh," I said.

I wrapped up the conversation and then I had to give Haig a *Reader's Digest* version of it. Then he told me what I had to do next, and I made some notes in my notebook and headed for the door.

Tulip walked me to the door. When we were out of Haig's hearing range she slipped an arm around my waist. She turned her body so that her breasts rubbed companionably against my chest.

"Not enough sex," she purred. "Ho, boy! How about a fast bourbon and yogurt?"

I'm sure I blushed that time. Damn it.

* * *

I got the Cadillac from the garage. It's my car, but if it weren't for Haig I wouldn't be able to go on owning it. He pays fifty dollars a month so that it can live in a garage on Tenth Avenue. Maybe twice a year I have occasion to use it, and yes, it would be a lot cheaper to rent a car, but I like this one and Haig doesn't seem to mind the expense. The car was given to me by Geraldine, who runs a whorehouse in Bordentown, South Carolina, where I worked for a while as a deputy sheriff.

(You could read about it if you want. It's in a book called *Chip Harrison Scores Again.* I want you to know that the title was not my idea.)

Anyway, the car's a Cadillac, which sounds impressive, but it's also more than twenty years old, and I guess it's the last stick-shift automobile that Cadillac ever made. It's in beautiful shape, though. Geraldine only drove it on Sundays. To church and back.

I picked it up at the garage, crossed over to Jersey and managed to find the Palisades Parkway. I got off at the Alpine exit and found the town of Closter, and I only had to ask directions four times before I found Haskell Henderson's house. It was a colonial, painted yellow with forest green trim, set fairly far back on a lot shaded by a great many large trees. A huge dog in a fenced yard next door barked at me. I waved at him and walked up a flagstone path to the front door and poked the bell. An elaborate series of chimes sounded within the house. I waited for a while and was about to hit the bell again when the door opened. A woman stood in the doorway with a cigarette in one hand and a glass of colorless liquid in the other. She said, "If you're from the Boy Scouts, the newspapers are stacked in the garage. If you're from the ecology drive the bottles and cans are in a bin next to the newspapers. If you're selling something I've probably already got it and it doesn't work and the last thing I want is to buy another one."

I was standing close enough during her little speech to identify the colorless liquid in her glass. It was gin. Mrs. Haskell Henderson was in her early thirties, built like the Maginot Line, and already sloshed to the gills at ten twenty-five in the morning.

"I'm not," I said.

"You're not which?"

"Any of them," I said. "My name is Chip Harrison and I work for Leo Haig."

"I don't."

"I beg your pardon?"

"I don't work for Leo Haig. I don't work for anybody. My name is Althea Henderson and I drink a lot. And why shouldn't I, huh? That's what I want to know."

"Well. May I come in?"

"What the hell, why not." She stood aside and I entered the house. "Why shouldn't I drink?" she demanded. "Kids are at camp, husband's at the office, why shouldn't I drink?" She gestured vaguely and some of the gin moved abruptly from the glass to the oriental rug. She didn't appear to notice. "Bad for the liver," she said. "Well, what the hell do I care, huh? Who wants to drop dead and leave a perfectly good liver behind? What you got to do in this world is wear out all at once. It's a question of timing."

"Oh."

"Wanna drink?"

"It's a little early for me, thanks."

"Then how 'bout some carrot juice? Carrot juice, papaya juice, dandelion coffee—that's the kind of crap my husband drinks. How 'bout a nice bowlful of sprouted alfalfa, huh? Just the thing to set you up for a hard day's work, right?"

"Speaking of your husband, Mrs. Henderson—"

"Call me Althea."

"Speaking of your husband, Althea—"

"What about him?" Her eyes narrowed, and I got the impression she wasn't quite as drunk as she made out. She'd been drinking, certainly, and it was getting to her, but she had been riding it a little, either for my benefit or because it felt good. "What about him? Is he in some kind of trouble?"

"It's possible."

"It's that girl who was murdered, isn't it? The one with the big tits."

"Cherry Bounce, yes."

"Cherry Bounce my ass," she said. "That little bitch

must have given her cherry the bounce when she was eleven years old. Was he fucking her?"

"No."

"That's a surprise. Maybe her tits weren't big enough. Were they big ones?"

"Well. Uh. Yes, uh, they were."

"Then I'm surprised he could keep his hands off them," she said. She took another swig of gin and asked if I was sure I didn't want to drink. I was sure, and said so. "He's a tit man, Haskell is. Always has been. A health freak and a tit freak. That's why he runs around the way he does. Oh, hell, if you were thinking about keeping his secret, he hasn't got any secret to keep. The two of us play a game. He pretends I don't know he runs around and I pretend the same, but all it is is a game."

She flopped into a chair. "He can't fool me. All the health crap he eats, all the vitamins he takes, the man's got more energy than Con Edison. He used to make it with me twice a night and once every morning. Rain or shine, three times a day. He was wearing me out. And now he hasn't made it with me in almost three years."

I didn't say anything.

"Because of these," she said, cupping her enormous breasts in her hands.

"I don't get it."

"Neither do I," she said. "Used to get it three times a

day and now I don't get it at all. Because of these. They used to be the reason he married me, and now—"

"Uh—"

"The hell of it is that I love the bastard. And he loves me. But I don't turn him on anymore. Because he's a tit man and that's all there is to it."

"You lost me," I said.

She stood up. "C'mere," she said. I stepped closer to her. She put the index finger of her right hand to the tip of her left breast. "Feel," she said. "Christ sake, don't just stand there. Grab yourself a handful. Go on, dammit!"

I cupped her breast with my hand.

"Don't be shy. Give it a little squeeze."

I gave it a little squeeze.

"Feel good?"

"Uh, yes."

"Now the other one."

"Look, Mrs. Henderson—"

"Althea, dammit."

"Look, Althea—"

"Shut up. Feel the other one, will you?"

I followed orders.

"Well?"

"Well what?"

"Uh—"

"Both feel the same?"

"Sure."

"Not from this end they don't. Wait right here.

Don't go away." I waited right there and didn't go away and she came back with a hat pin about four inches long. "Stick it in my tit," she said. "The left one."

"Don't be ridiculous. Look, Mrs. Henderson, Althea, maybe I should come back some other time. I—"

"Oh, hell," she said, and plunged the hatpin into her left breast. My stomach flipped a little but she didn't seem to feel a thing. She drew out the pin. There was no blood on it. Her eyes challenged me and I began to get the picture.

"Foam rubber," she said. "The other one's real. Until a couple of years ago they were both real and Haskell was crazy about them. Then I had to have a mastectomy because some knife-happy surgeon decided I had the big C. Turned out it was benign but by that time he'd already done his cutting. Only half a woman now. Used to turn Haskell on. Now all I turn him is off. Still loves me, I still love him, but he takes all his vitamins and drinks his carrot juice and eats his alfalfa and walks around horny as a toad and I don't do him any good. That's why he needs his topless dancers."

I stood there wondering why floors never open up and swallow you when you want them to. She went out to the kitchen for more gin. I thought she was lucky she wasn't too drunk when she did her trick with the hatpin or she might get the wrong breast by mistake and it would probably hurt. When she came back I managed to steer the conversation back in its

original direction. I asked her what she had been doing the night before last, and what her husband had
been doing.

"He was working late at the store," she said. "Do
you believe that?"

"Well—"

"And I was drinking carrot juice and counting my
nipples. Do you believe that?"

"Althea—"

"He was chasing women in New York. And I was
here, sitting in front of the television set and drinking
scotch. Not gin. I never drink gin after four in the
afternoon. Only a pansy would drink gin after four in
the afternoon."

"I see. Can you prove it?"

"Prove it? Hell, everybody knows only a pansy
would drink gin in the nighttime. What's there to
prove?"

"Can you prove you were home watching
television?"

"Oh," she said. She thought it over. "You think I
went into New York and stuck a pin in that girl's tit.
What was her name again?"

"Cherry Bounce."

"Why the hell would I do a thing like that? I don't
go around sticking pins in tits all the time like some
kind of a nut. I just did it now to prove a point. Lessee.
Kids are at camp so they can't gimme an alibi. Oh,
sure. My neighbor from down the street was over

here. Got here about nine o'clock, left when Johnny Carson went off the air. Marge Whitman, lives just down the street. She's in the same boat as me. Well, not exactly. She's got two tits but she's got a pansy for a husband. Leaves her out here and spends his night picking up sailors on Times Square, the fucking pansy. Drinks gin all night long, the goddamn fruit."

I got the Whitman woman's address and started backing toward the door. She asked me where I was going. "I have some other calls to make," I said.

"I turn you off too, don't I?"

"No, not at all, but—"

"You're a tit man like my husband."

"Not exactly."

"You don't like tits?"

"I like them fine, but—"

"You're not a pansy, are you?" I shook my head. "What do you drink in the evening?"

"Whiskey, usually. Sometimes a beer. Why?"

"Not a pansy," she said. And then she took her blouse off, and then she took her bra off, and I just stood there. She had one absolutely perfect breast, and where the other had been there was smooth skin with an almost imperceptible scar from the incision.

"Sickening, isn't it?"

"No, not at all."

"Deformed."

"No."

"Turns you off, doesn't it?"

The weird thing is that it was turning me on. I don't know how to account for it and I'd rather not stop and figure it out. It probably just proves I'm kinkier than I realized, but why go into it too closely?

"C'mere," she said. I did, and she opened my zipper and groped around. "I'll be a sonofabitch," she said. "Well, you're not a faggot, are you?"

"No, and—"

"And I don't turn you off, do I? Maybe you're a sensible tit man, that's what it must be. You figure half a loaf is better than none. Right?"

"Uh."

Her hand clutched me possessively. She turned and began leading me toward the staircase. I had the choice of following her or leaving part of my anatomy behind, and I've always been attached to it. I followed.

If Althea had had her way she would have kept me there for hours. And I'll tell you something. If we weren't in the middle of a case I would have stayed. She evidently had an enormous complex about her absent breast, which old Haskell must have done a good job of reinforcing, and as a result she did everything she could to compensate for what she regarded as a terrible deficiency. As far as I was concerned, passing her up because she only had one breast was like refusing to listen to Schubert's Eighth Symphony because he never got around to finishing it.

I finally managed to get out of there after promising

to return when I got the chance. Then I stopped at the Whitman house to confirm Althea's alibi, although I didn't really need confirmation. But Haig would be sure to ask and I would have to have the answers.

Mrs. Whitman was quick to recall watching television with Althea on the night in question. She was also quick to offer me a cup of coffee, which I declined because I was really in a hurry. And I got the impression that she would have gladly offered me a lot more than coffee. She was a good looking woman, a little older than Althea, but certainly nothing to complain about.

Back in the car, I wondered if Mr. Whitman was really homosexual. The fact that he drank gin in the evening didn't strike me as sufficient evidence in and of itself. I know a lot of perfectly straight people who drink gin in the evening. I think they're crazy, but it doesn't make them gay.

Then I began thinking about the conversation with Clover, and how I'd told her there probably wouldn't be much sex in the book. I wondered if our talk had had anything to do with the fact that Althea and I wound up in bed. I suppose it could have operated on a sort of subliminal level. Maybe it was my aspirations as an author that goaded me to respond to Althea's advances.

Somehow I doubt it.

* * *

I drove back over the George Washington Bridge and down the West Side Drive. I got off at 72nd Street and drove down to Tulip's building. Of course there was no place to park. I circled a few blocks a few times and then stuck it in a lot. The attendant was very impressed by the car and flipped completely when he saw he was going to have to shift it. "A Cad with a stick shift," he said. "Where'd you ever find it?"

"South Carolina."

"There a lot of 'em down there?"

"Thousands," I said.

On the way to Tulip's building I spent a dime on a telephone and made my report. It took some time and I had to feed the phone extra change. I left out the part about going to bed with Althea. Verbatim only goes so far is the way I figure it.

Haig told me it was satisfactory. I was glad to hear it. He said, "After you see Miss Tattersall, you'll go to Tulip's apartment and feed her fish. You have the key?"

"Yes, sir. She gave it to me a couple of hours ago. You told her to, remember?"

"The *Ctenapoma* receive brine shrimp. There's some in the freezer compartment of the refrigerator. I believe that's all they receive. One moment."

He asked Tulip if this was so, and she said there were also some bloodworms and mealworms in jars in the refrigerator, and I should give them that if it was no trouble. "They're strictly carnivores," I heard her say. "Unless—I wonder if that's what's keeping them from spawning! I used to give the scats a lot of wheat germ and it put them in great breeding condition."

Haig said, "Chip."

"Yes."

He covered the mouth piece with his hand and I couldn't make out what he and Tulip were saying to each other. Then he said, "There is a jar of Kretchmer wheat germ in the cupboard to the right of the sink. On the second or third shelf, Miss Wolinski doesn't recall precisely where."

"I'll manage to find it. You want me to give some to the *Ctenapoma*?"

"No! Absolutely not."

"Fine. Hold your horses. Then what difference does it make what shelf it's on?"

"Bring the wheat germ back here with you. Do not open the jar. Be very careful of the jar. Wrap it so that it won't break should you happen to drop it. Do you understand?"

"Oh."

"Do you understand, Chip?"

"I think so," I said. "I think I do."

Fifteen

HAIG MAKES ME read a lot of mysteries. Since we don't get all that many cases, and since you can only spend so much time feeding fish and cleaning out filters, that leaves me with plenty of time to humor him. It's his theory that you can learn anything and solve any puzzle if you just read enough mystery novels. Maybe he's right. It certainly seems to work for him, but he's a genius and I feel that constitutes special circumstances.

Well, if you've read as many of them as I have—not even as many as Haig has, because nobody has read that many—then you know what happened when I finally got around to seeing Helen Tattersall. I mean, her name came up early on, and I kept ducking opportunities to see her, so naturally one of two things had to happen. Either she turned out to be the killer or she supplied the one missing piece of information that tied the whole mess together. Right?

Wrong. Absolutely wrong.

I got in to see her by posing as someone investigating her complaint about her neighbors. Even then I had a hard time because she really didn't like the idea of opening her door, but I explained that I couldn't act on the complaint unless I interviewed her face-to-face. Much as she didn't want to open her door, she decided to risk it if it would facilitate her making trouble for somebody.

When she opened the door I decided on my own that she hadn't gone to Treasure Chest and planted a poisoned dart in Cherry Bounce's breast. Because Helen Tattersall was in a wheelchair with her leg in a cast, and the first thing she did was inform me that she'd been in the cast for two months and expected to be in it for another four months, and she didn't sound very happy about it.

The next thing she said was, "Now which complaint have you come about? The upstairs neighbors? Those prostitutes? Or the man next door who plays the flute all day and all night? Or the married couple on the other side of me with that dreadful squalling baby? Or the man across the hall who gives me dirty looks? Or the evil man down by the elevator who puts poison gas in everybody's air-conditioners? Or could it be my complaints about the building employees? The superintendent is a Soviet agent, you know—"

So she didn't even have a personal vendetta against

Tulip and Cherry. Instead she had just one enemy: mankind. And she complained about and tried to make trouble for every member of the human race who called himself to her attention.

Well, I couldn't get out of there fast enough. I began wishing I were Richard Widmark in *Kiss of Death* so that I could push the old bitch down a staircase, wheelchair and all. I'm not saying I would have done it, but I might have given it serious consideration.

I suppose there should have been one little thing she said that got my mind working in the right direction, one little thread she might unwittingly supply, but I'm sorry, there just wasn't anything like that. It was a waste of time. I had sort of thought it would be a waste of time, and that's why I'd postponed seeing Helen Tattersall as long as I did, in addition to having suspected that meeting her wouldn't be one of my all-time favorite experiences. I was right on all counts, and it was a pleasure to get out of her apartment, believe me.

I found a staircase and climbed a flight to Tulip's apartment and used her key to open her door. I got a rush when I walked in, remembering how I had let myself into Andrew Mallard's apartment the previous evening, and half-expecting to find another corpse or two now. I don't guess I really thought that would happen, but I have to admit I went around touching things with the heel of my hand to avoid leaving fingerprints.

No corpses, thank God. Not in the fish tank, either. The two *Ctenapoma fasciolatum* swam around on either side of their glass divider. They were doing a great job of ignoring each other, and the male had done absolutely nothing about building a bubble nest.

I sat on the edge of the bed and watched them for a while. "C'mon," I said at one point. "Clover Swann wants plenty of sex in this book, gang. You can't expect me to supply all of it myself, can you?"

I don't think they cared.

So I gave up on them and went into the kitchen. I found brine shrimp in the freezer and broke off a chunk, and I found containers of bloodworms and mealworms in the fridge. I went back to the bedroom and fed them until they wouldn't eat any more, then returned the food to the kitchen. I opened a couple of cupboards until I spotted the jar of wheat germ. I reached for it, and then I stopped with my hand halfway to it, and I told myself not to be silly, fingerprints never solved anything anyway and all that, and then I got a paper towel and used it to take the jar from the shelf and set it on the counter top. There wouldn't be any useful prints and I knew it, but if Haig did check the jar for prints and found mine all over it I would never hear the end of it.

I wrapped the jar in several thicknesses of paper

towels and found a paper bag in another cupboard and put the jar in that. Then I left it in the kitchen and took a careful look around the apartment without knowing what I was looking for.

I suppose the police must have tossed the place fairly thoroughly the night of the murder, but I had to credit them with doing a neat job of it. As far as I could tell nothing was out of place.

I went into Cherry's room, and of course it was impossible to tell whether anything was out of place there or not, because nothing had been in place to begin with. I remember standing there just two days ago when the only victims had been scats, remembered thinking that Cherry was evidently something of a slob, and now I found myself muttering an apology to her. I guess a girl can throw her underwear around the room if she wants to. I guess it's her own business.

We'll get him, I promised her. I don't know who he is, and I don't know if Haig knows who he is, but we'll get the bastard.

I tucked the jar of wheat germ under my arm and got out of there. The guy at the parking lot ground the Caddy's gears a little but it didn't sound as though he'd done any permanent damage. I gave him a quarter and drove back to our garage and turned the car over to Emilio, who never grinds the gears, and who occasionally polishes it when he has nothing else to do. We don't pay him to polish the Cadillac. He does it because he likes to.

Then I tucked the jar of wheat germ under my arm again and walked back to Haig's house.

Sixteen

I WANTED TO get up a pool on who would be the first to arrive. But Haig wouldn't play. At a quarter to three he sent Tulip to the guest room and ordered her to stay there until he called for her. After she was tucked away he and I discussed the seating arrangements. I hate having to tell people where to sit, although I have to admit it usually works out fairly well. You can take a person into a room with twenty chairs in it, tell him he's expected to sit in one specific one, and it's a rare case when he gives you an argument. I suppose that proves we're a nation of sheep just looking to be led, but I'm not sure about that. I figure people are just relieved to be saved the aggravation of making an unimportant decision.

At twenty minutes to three Haig went upstairs to ask the fish who killed Cherry Bounce. I hoped they would tell him because it was going to be awfully embarrassing if he ran the whole number and nothing happened. I don't know whether he had it all worked out at that point or not. I figured the reason he went upstairs was so that he would be able to make a grand entrance after they were all seated and waiting for him.

Anyway, I would have been glad to get up a pool, and I would have lost. My pick was Haskell Henderson, and I had a reason for picking him, but since I was wrong there's no point in going into the reason. The first person to show rang the doorbell at four minutes of three. I passed the kitchen on my way to the door and exchanged glances with Wong. "Here we go," I said, and he said something in his native tongue, and I opened the door. There was a man standing on the welcome mat whom I had never seen before in my life.

He had a very youthful face if you didn't spot the pouches under the eyes or the lines at their corners. His hair was the color of sand, neither long nor short, and his eyes were as clear a blue as I have ever seen. He had an open friendly Van Johnson kind of face. He was wearing a gray plaid suit and his tie, loose around his neck, was a striped job.

He said, "I have an appointment with a Mr. Haig."

"You're in luck," I said. "We have a Mr. Haig who will probably fit the bill very nicely. Your name is Glenn Flatt and you're early."

He stared at me. He looked as though he had had his next line of dialogue prepared days in advance and

I had blown his timing with an ad lib. I told him to come in, closed the door, and led him to the office. Wong and I had set up a double row of chairs on my side of the partner's desk, facing Haig's chair. I showed Flatt which chair was his and he sat, then popped up again as if there had been a tack on the seat.

"Just a minute," he said. "I don't understand any of this. I came here because I wanted to help Mr. Haig. He said he was working on my ex-wife's behalf and I wanted to help him. Where is he?"

"He's busy," I said. "He'll be along in a while. That's your chair but you don't have to sit in it if you don't want to. You can look at the fish if you'd rather."

"Fish," he said.

I was waiting for him to ask me who I was, but he didn't. I guess he didn't care. Nor did he look at the fish. He sat down again, opened his briefcase, and took out a copy of the *Post*. He opened it to Jack Anderson's column and checked out the current entry in the corruption sweepstakes. I sat in my chair for a minute or two but it got to be sort of heavy, just the two of us in a roomful of empty chairs, so I went into the kitchen and watched Wong sharpen his cleaver.

The next two customers showed up together, and neither of them was Haskell Henderson, so I lost the place and show money too. They were Simon Barckover and Maeve O'Connor. Maeve looked bubbly and radiant and beautiful and Barckover looked pissed off.

"What's this all about?" he demanded. "I'm a busy

man. I've got things to do. Who does this Leo Haig think he is? Where does he get off ordering me to come here?"

There were just too many questions so I didn't answer any of them. I told him he was absolutely right, which gave him pause, and I led the two of them into the office and showed them to their seats. They looked at Glenn Flatt and he looked at them, and then he went back to his newspaper and Barckover sat staring straight ahead while Maeve went and looked at some fish.

After that they all started to show up, and I kept scurrying back and forth from the door to the office, ignoring questions and mumbling inane replies and getting everybody in the right seats. First Haskell Henderson showed up, looking about the same as yesterday but twice as nervous. He'd changed from white jeans to dove-gray jeans, but the goatee was still scraggly and he was wearing either the same Doctor Ecology tee-shirt or one just like it. I no sooner got him parked than Gus Leemy came along with Buddy Lippa in tow. Neither of them said a word, and when I brought them into the office they acted as if they were entering an empty room. They took their seats without acknowledging the presence of any of the others in any way whatsoever.

As far as that goes, there was a lot of mutual ignoring going on in the office. A lot of these people had met before, but evidently they had managed to piece out the fact that Haig intended to expose a murderer, which meant that one of them was due to be the ex-posee, and I guess they didn't quite know how to re-late to that. It was fine with me, just so they stayed in their chairs and didn't make waves.

Jan Remo came next, asking if she was late. I told her she was right on time, and as I was leading her to the office the bell rang again. I hurried her in and came back to admit Rita Cubbage. She wasn't wearing the wig this time and her tight Afro cap was a significant improvement. "Much better," I told her, taking a long look. "You ought to give that wig to the boss. Your boss, not mine. He's bald as an egg and it might be an improvement. Did you remember what it was that you couldn't quite remember last night?"

"I dreamed something," she said. She opened her purse and took out a slip of paper. "And when I woke up this was on the bedside table, but I don't recall writing it down."

I took the slip of paper from her. On it, in a very pre-cise handwriting that no one would be capable of managing in the middle of the night, she had written: *"Some white boys can be fun to sleep with."*

"I do wish I recalled that dream," she said. "It must have been a good one."

"I wish I'd been there."

"Just might be that you were," she said.

I opened my mouth, and then I closed my mouth, and then I seated her and came back in time to open the door for Leonard Danzig. There was a man on either side of him, and they were the very same men who had taken hold of my arms the night before. I was trying to decide how to tell them they couldn't come in when he turned to them and told them to wait outside, which made things a whole lot simpler for me.

"Well," he said. "Everything proceeding on schedule?"

"So far."

"And your boss is going to make it all come together, is that right?"

"That's the plan."

"Well, if he makes it work, I'll pay off on the spot." He tapped the breast pocket of his suit, indicating that he'd brought the money along. "If I owe somebody something, I see to it that the debt is paid."

A sort of chill grabbed me when he said that. He was talking about money, about paying money if he owed it, but I had the feeling that I never wanted him to owe me something else. Like a bullet in the head, for example. Because I was sure he'd pay that debt just as promptly, and with the same kind of satisfaction.

I took him into the office and parked him, and there were two seats left, one on either side of the second row. I went into the kitchen, picked up the phone and buzzed the fourth floor.

"All but two," I said.

"Who hasn't arrived?"

"The twins. New York's Finest."

"They'll be here within five minutes. Buzz me when they arrive."

They were on hand within three minutes, and they were not happy to see me. "I don't like any of this," Gregorio informed me. "If Haig has something he should tell us. If he's got nothing he should stop wasting our time. If he wants to put on a performance let him hire a hall."

"Sure," I said. "That's his plan, actually. He's going to play the title role in *Tiny Alice*. Let's face it, you're here because this case has you up a tree and you figure Haig's going to hold the ladder for you. Either he'll get your murderer or he won't, and either way is fine with you. You wind up with a case solved or you get to see Haig fall on his face."

"I'd like that," Seidenwall said.

"You probably would but I don't think he's going to oblige you. Now you know the rules. You take your seats and you let Leo Haig run the show. This is his house and you're here by invitation. Understood?"

I swear the best part of my job is getting to talk to cops that way now and then. It makes it all worthwhile. They didn't like to put up with it, but they knew they didn't have any choice. I showed them their chairs, putting Gregorio on the far side of the room and Seidenwall nearest to the door. That way anyone who tried to leave in a hurry would have to go through Seidenwall, and I wouldn't want to try that myself unless I was driving a tank.

Let me go over the seating for you, in case you care. *I* don't, but it's one of the things Haig insists on.

The desk was where it always was, with Haig's chair behind it and mine in front of it and an armchair alongside of it, presently empty.

Then two rows of chairs facing the desk. In the first row, from the far side, were Leonard Danzig, Rita Cubbage, Glenn Flatt, Maeve O'Connor, and Simon Barckover. In the back row we had Detective Vincent Gregorio, Haskell Henderson, Gus Leemy, Buddy Lippa, Jan Remo, and Detective Wallace Seidenwall. I looked at them and decided they were a reasonably attractive group, well-mannered and neatly groomed. Leemy was wearing a business suit instead of a tuxedo so he didn't look like a penguin today, and Buddy wasn't wearing a sport jacket at all so he had nothing to clash with his slacks and shirt, but otherwise they looked about the same as always. I wished they would fold their hands on the tops of their desks and wait for the teacher to come and write something adorable on the blackboard.

I buzzed Haig from the kitchen. Then I went back to the office and sat down in my chair, and a minute or so later our client entered the room. Our original client, that is. Tulip. She took the armchair alongside the desk without being told.

Then Haig walked in and sat behind his desk and every eye in the room was drawn to him.

Including mine.

Seventeen

FOR A LONG moment he just sat there looking at them. His eyes scanned the room carefully. I thought I saw the hint of a smile for a second, but then it was gone and his round face maintained a properly stern and serious look. He put his hands on top of the desk, selected a pipe, put it back in the rack, and drew a breath.

"Good afternoon," he said. "I want to thank you all for coming. All but one of you are welcome in this house. That one is not welcome, but his presence is essential. One of you is a murderer. One of you is responsible for one hundred twenty-five deaths."

There was a collective gasp at that figure but he went on without appearing to notice. "All but two of those deaths were the deaths of fish. The penalty which society attaches to ichthyicide is minimal. Malicious mischief, perhaps. Certainly a misdemeanor. The other two victims were human, however. One would be difficult to substantiate as homicide. While I am mortally certain that Andrew Mallard was murdered—"

"Hey, wait a minute," Gregorio cut in. "If you've got any information on that you've been holding it out, and—"

"Mr. Gregorio." Gregorio stopped in midsentence. "I have withheld nothing, sir. I remind you again that you are here by invitation." He scanned the room again, then went on. "To continue. While I may be certain that Mr. Mallard was murdered, and while I could explain how the murder was committed, no jury would convict anyone for that murder. Indeed, no district attorney in his right mind would presume to bring charges. But the other murder, that of Miss Abramowicz, was unquestionably a case of premeditated homicide. The killer is in this room, and I intend to see him hang for it."

He'd have a long wait. While Haig longs for a return of capital punishment, and thinks public hanging was a hell of a fine way to run a society, the bulk of contemporary opinion seems to be flowing in the other direction.

"The day before yesterday," he said, "Miss Thelma Wolinski sought my assistance. An entire tank of young *Scatophagus tetracanthus* plus her breeder fish had died suddenly and of no apparent cause. Miss Wolinski is possessed of a scientific temperament. She had a chemical analysis of the aquarium water performed, and the laboratory certified that the water had been poisoned with strychnine. Miss Wolinski could not imagine why anyone would want to kill her generally inoffensive fish. She concluded that the crime was the work of a madman, that an attack upon her fish represented hostility toward her own person, and that she herself might consequently be in danger."

"She should have called the police," Seidenwall said.

Haig glared at him. "Indeed," he said. "No doubt you would have rushed to investigate the poisoning of a tankful of fish. Miss Wolinski is no witling." Seidenwall winced at the word. "She came to me. She could scarcely have made a wiser decision."

That sounded a little pompous to me, but nobody's hackles rose as far as I could tell. I looked at Tulip. I couldn't tell what she was thinking. She looked beautiful, and quite spectacular, but then she always did.

"Of course I agreed to investigate. That was quite proper on my part, but it also precipitated a murder. That very evening Miss Mabel Abramowicz was murdered. Some of you may know her as Cherry Bounce. She was killed while performing at a nightclub. Your nightclub, Mr. Leemy."

"Not my fault. I run a decent place."

"That is moot, and a non sequitur in the bargain. Miss Abramowicz was also poisoned, but not with strychnine. She was killed with curare, a lethal paralytic poison with which certain South American savages tip their arrows."

Haig picked up his pipe again and took it apart. He looked at the two pieces, and for a moment I thought that was all he had and he was waiting for a miracle. We'd be out four grand and I wouldn't get to write a book.

"It was instantly evident that the deaths of the fish and the death of Miss Abramowicz were related. It was furthermore a working hypothesis that the same person was responsible for both outrages. Finally, it seemed more than coincidence that Miss Abramowicz's death followed so speedily upon Miss Wolinski's engaging me to represent her interests. Once I was working on the case, Miss Abramowicz had to be disposed of as rapidly as possible. Had the time element not been of paramount importance, the murderer would not have had to take the great risk of committing his crime in full view of perhaps a hundred people.

"And it was an enormous risk, to be sure. But our murderer was very fortunate. While I have never met her, my associate Mr. Harrison assures me that Miss Abramowicz's endowments were such as to make her the center of attention during her performance. Everyone watched her as her act neared its climax. No one saw—or, more accurately, no one paid attention to—her murderer.

"With one exception, I would submit. Andrew Mallard saw something. He may not have known what he saw. He was clearly not certain enough or self-assured enough to make any mention of his observations to the police. Whether this testifies to Mr. Mallard's lethargy and reticence or to the inefficiency of police interrogation is beside the point. In any event—"

"I'll pretend I didn't hear that," Gregorio said.

"An excellent policy," Haig murmured. "In any event, the murderer struck, the murder weapon was not recovered, and the murderer seemed to be in the clear."

The projectile, I thought. Not the weapon.

"A surface examination would suggest that the murderer was irrational. Item: He poisons Miss Wolinski's fish with strychnine. Item: He poisons Miss Abramowicz with curare. The two incidents cannot fail to be related, yet how are they linked in the mind of the murderer? I must admit that, after I learned of Mr. Mallard's death, there was a moment when I entertained the hypothesis that the murderer was attempting to strike at Miss Wolinski by destroying everything associated with her—first her pets, then her roommate, finally a former lover. I dismissed this possibility almost at once. I returned to the fish. I decided to assume the killer was rational, and I asked myself why a rational killer would poison fish with strychnine.

"The answer was that he would not. If he wished to kill the fish and make it obvious that he had done so, he might have tipped over their aquarium and let them perish gasping upon the floor. If he wished to make the death look accidental he could have caused their demise in any of a dozen ways which would not have aroused any suspicion. Instead he chose a readily detectable poison without having any grounds for assuming that Miss Wolinski would bother to detect it via chemical analysis.

"The conclusion was obvious. The fish had been killed by mistake. The murderer did not put the strychnine into the aquarium."

Tulip frowned. "Then who did?"

"Ah," Haig said. He turned to her, a gentle smile on his round face. "I'm afraid you did, Miss Wolinski. Unwittingly, you poisoned your own fish."

Tulip gaped at him. I looked around the room to check out the reactions of the audience. They ran the gamut from puzzlement to disinterest. Seidenwall looked as though he might drop off to sleep any minute now. Gregorio seemed to be enduring all of this, waiting for Haig either to make his point or wind up with egg on his face. I tried to find a suspect who indicated that he or she already knew how the strychnine got in the tank. I didn't have a clue.

Haig opened a desk drawer and took out a paper bag that looked familiar. Gingerly he extracted the jar of wheat germ from it and peeled away the protective layers of paper toweling. He wrapped a towel around his hand and pushed the jar toward my side of the desk.

"This is a jar of wheat germ," he said. "I have found it to be an excellent dietary supplement for fishes. I am told it is similarly useful for human beings. I have no grounds for confirming or disputing the latter. Mr. Henderson. Do you recognize this jar? You may examine it closely, but I urge you not to touch it."

Henderson shrugged. "I don't need a close look," he said. "It's Kretchmer, one of the standard brands. They sell it all over the place, supermarkets, everywhere. What about it?"

"Do they also sell it in health food emporia?"

"Sometimes."

"I understand you run a chain of such establishments. Do your stores carry Kretchmer wheat germ?"

"I think so."

"You don't know for certain, Mr. Henderson?"

"As a matter of fact we do carry it. Why not? It's a good brand, we move a lot of cases of it."

"Do you recognize this particular jar, Mr. Henderson?"

"They're all the same. If you're asking did it come from my place, I couldn't tell you one way or the other."

"I could," Haig said. "On the reverse of this jar there is a label. It says 'Doctor Ecology' and there is an address beneath the store name. That label would tend to suggest that this jar of wheat germ came from one of your stores."

"Well, then it must have. What's the point?"

Haig ignored the question. He picked up the bell and rang it, and Wong Fat came in carrying a two-quart goldfish bowl. There were a pair of inch-and-a-half common goldfish in the bowl. Haig buys them from Aquarium Stock Company for $4.75 a hundred and feeds them to larger fish that have to have live fish as food. Wong put the bowl on the desk. I wondered if it was going to leave a ring.

His hand covered with a paper towel, Haig screwed the top off the jar. He reached into the jar with a little spoon he used to use to clean the crud out of his pipes back in the days when he was trying to smoke them. He spooned up a few grains of wheat germ and sprinkled them into the goldfish bowl.

The fish swam around for a few seconds, not knowing they'd been fed. They weren't enormously bright. Then they surfaced and began scoffing down the wheat germ.

"Now watch," Haig said.

We all watched, and we didn't have to watch for very long before both fish were floating belly-up on the surface. They did not look to be in perfect health.

"They are dead," Haig said. "As dead as the *Scatophagus tetracanthus*. As dead as Miss Mabel Abramowicz. I have not had a chemical analysis run on the contents of this jar of wheat germ. It does seem reasonable to assume that the wheat germ is laced with strychnine. Miss Wolinski."

"Yes?"

"How did this jar of wheat germ come into your possession?"

"Haskell gave it to me."

Henderson's eyes were halfway out of his head. Alfalfa sprouts or no, he looked as though a coronary occlusion was just around the corner. "Now wait a minute," he said. "You just wait a goddamned minute now."

"You deny having given this jar to Miss Wolinski?"

"I sure as hell deny putting strychnine in it. Maybe that's the jar I gave her and maybe it isn't. How the hell do I know?"

"You did give her a jar, however?"

"I gave her lots of things."

"Indeed. You gave her a jar of wheat germ?"

"Yeah, I guess so."

"Have you any reason to assume this is other than the jar you gave her?"

"How the hell do I know?" Haig glared at him. "Okay," he said. "It's probably the same jar."

Haig nodded, satisfied. "Miss Wolinski. Was Mr. Henderson in the habit of gifting you with health foods?"

"Yes."

"And what did you do with them?"

Tulip lowered her eyes. "I didn't do anything with them," she said.

"You didn't eat them?"

"No." She shrugged, and when you're built like Tulip a shrug is a hell of a gesture. "I know that kind of food is supposed to be good for you," she said, "but

I just don't *like* it. I like things like hamburgers and french fries and beer, things like that."

"If you would just *try* them—" Henderson began.

"Mr. Henderson. Had Miss Wolinski tried the wheat germ she would be dead." Henderson shut up. "Miss Wolinski," Haig went on pleasantly. "You did nothing with the health foods? You merely put them aside?"

"Well, I used to feed the wheat germ to the fish some of the time. It's a good conditioner for breeding."

"It is indeed. I employ it myself. What else became of the health foods Mr. Henderson was considerate enough to give to you?"

"Sometimes Cherry ate them."

"Indeed," Haig said. He got to his feet. "At this point things begin to clarify themselves. The strychnine was introduced into the aquarium not by the murderer but by Miss Wolinski herself. And it was added to the wheat germ not in an attempt to kill fish but in an attempt to kill Miss Abramowicz. Oh, sit down, Mr. Henderson. Do sit down. I am not accusing you of presenting Miss Wolinski with poisoned wheat germ. You are neither that stupid nor that clever. The strychnine was added to the wheat germ after it had come into Miss Wolinski's possession, added by someone who knew that Miss Abramowicz rather than Miss Wolinski was likely to ingest it. Sit *down!*"

Haskell Henderson sat down. I decided Haig was wrong on one point. Old Haskell was stupid enough to do almost anything. Anybody who would discontinue making love to Althea simply because she had less than the usual number of breasts didn't have all that much going for him in the brains department.

Haig turned to Tulip once more. "Miss Wolinski," he said. "I first made your acquaintance approximately forty-eight hours ago. They have been eventful hours, to be sure. When did you decide to consult me?"

"Tuesday. The day after I got the lab report. That was when I decided, and then I thought it over for a while, and then I came here."

"Who knew of your decision?"

"Nobody."

"No one at all?"

"I didn't tell anyone after I saw you. You told me not to. Oh, wait a minute. I said something to Cherry that morning, that I was going to see you and you would find out how it happened."

"So you told Miss Abramowicz. And she might have told anyone."

"Cherry wasn't very good at keeping things to herself."

"She may have told anyone at all," Haig went on. "What we do know for certain is that she told her murderer. He realized that I would rapidly determine that the poisoning of the scats constituted a misdirected attempt at Miss Abramowicz's life. He had to act quickly."

Haig cleared his throat and let his eyes take a tour of the audience. I don't know what he was looking for so I don't know whether or not he found it. What I saw was Rita Cubbage picking at a cuticle, Buddy Lippa scratching his head, Gus Leemy frowning, Vincent Gregorio picking lint off his lapel, Simon Barckover glancing at his watch, Maeve O'Connor licking her lower lip, Glenn Flatt cracking his knuckles, Jan Remo rubbing her temples with her fingertips, Wallace Seidenwall yawning, and Leonard Danzig sitting in perfect repose, giving Leo Haig every bit of his attention.

Whatever Haig was looking for and whether he found it or not, he evidently decided that the Rasboras were more interesting to look at than the eleven of them. He swung his chair around and stared into the fish tank, presenting his audience with a great view of the back of his head.

That's it, I thought. That's all he's got. I decided it was still pretty good, better than the police had managed to come up with, but why blow it by putting the show together prematurely? Unless he expected one of them to crack, but could you count on that happening? I decided you couldn't.

Haig swiveled his chair around again. "Mr. Flatt," he said. "Mr. Glenn Flatt."

There was a lot of head-turning as our customers tried to figure out which of them was Glenn Flatt. They finally took a cue from Haig and looked where he was looking, and the boyish Ivy Leaguer frowned back at Haig.

"Yes, I was hoping you'd get around to me," Flatt said. "I came here to help Tulip. I used to be married to her and we're still good friends and you said you were working for her. I didn't know I was going to be part of a carnival." He stood up. "I told you I had work to do. I came here as a favor to Tulip but this is ridiculous. I'm leaving."

"You are not. You will stay where you are. If you attempt to leave Mr. Harrison will knock you down and return you to your chair. Sit down, Mr. Flatt."

Flatt sat down, which took a load off my mind, believe me. If you think I was all that confident of my ability to knock him down you don't know me very well.

"Mr. Flatt. You came here because last evening I told you that I knew you were at Treasure Chest on the evening when Miss Abramowicz was murdered. That is why you are present this afternoon. When I told you I had a witness placing you at the scene you elected to cooperate."

"Where'd you get a witness?" Gregorio wanted to know. "And why did you hold that out?"

Haig made a face. "I had no witness," he said. "I merely said I had one."

"You were lying," Flatt said. It was a pretty dumb thing to say, and he sounded pretty dumb saying it.

"You might put it that way," Haig allowed. "Or you might say that I was bluffing. I trust you're conversant with the term, Mr. Flatt. You gamble quite a great deal, do you not?"

"Sometimes I'll make a bet on a horse."

"Indeed. Or on an athletic event, or on an election, or on the turn of a card. Would you say you are a compulsive gambler, Mr. Flatt?"

"Not in a million years," Flatt said. He looked somewhat less boyish now. "I like a little action, that's all. So I gamble. There's no law against it."

"Tommyrot. There are innumerable laws against various forms of gambling. The fact that such statutes are absurd does not wipe them from the criminal code. But we are not assembled here to convict you of gambling, Mr. Flatt. Rest assured of that."

"Look, I don't—"

Haig put his pipe back together again and tapped the bowl on the top of the desk. "I would be inclined to label you a compulsive gambler," he said. "The evidence seems clear enough. Your marriage to my client dissolved largely because you kept going into debt as a result of your gambling. Your debts have increased considerably over the years. A friend of mine was in a position to make inquiries among various bookmakers on Long Island. You are well known to several of them. You gamble heavily. You almost invariably lose."

"I don't do so badly."

"You do pay your debts," Haig said. "According to my information, in the past four months you paid an amount to bookmakers slightly in excess of your salary during the same period."

"That's ridiculous. And you couldn't possibly prove it."

"I don't have to. I told you I don't intend to convict you of gambling. And your gambling doesn't interfere with your ability to earn a livelihood, does it? You continue to be gainfully employed in a responsible position."

Flatt eyed him warily. "So?"

"As a pharmaceutical chemist, I understand."

"That's right."

"A position which would give you ready access to any number of interesting compounds. Such as strychnine and curare, to cite two examples."

"Now wait a goddamned minute—"

"Mr. Flatt, you're much better off if you keep your mouth shut. Take my word for it. You have access to such compounds and it would be puerile of you to deny it. That crossed my mind when first I learned of your occupation. Various poisons are readily obtainable. Strychnine is not. Neither is curare. You and I have not met before, Mr. Flatt, and we did not speak to one another until last evening, but you have been an important suspect since I first learned how the fish had died." He said all this in a calm conversational tone. Then abruptly he raised his voice to as close as he could come to a bellow. *Why were you at Treasure Chest the night before last?*

"You can't prove I was there."

"Phooey. You've already admitted you were there. Have the courage of your errors, Mr. Flatt. Why were you there?"

Flatt bought himself a couple of seconds by glancing to either side of himself. If he was looking for support he picked the wrong place to look for it. Everybody seemed to want to hear the answer to the question.

"I wasn't there when Cherry was killed," he said. "I left before her act started, I was miles away when she was killed. And I can prove it."

"That won't be necessary," Haig said. "You did not kill Miss Abramowicz."

"But—"

"Nor have you answered the question. Why did you go to that night club that evening?"

He shrugged. "No particular reason. I'm sorry if I was out of line but I thought you were accusing me of murder." He managed a boyish grin. "It certainly sounded that way for a while. For a little guy, you certainly know how to boss people around."

"You still haven't answered my question, Mr. Flatt."

"Oh, hell. Look, I wanted a couple of drinks. Why did I pick a topless club? Jesus, you know the answer to that one. Or maybe you don't, who knows with you? I like to look at girls. That's all there is to it. I used to be married to Tulip and we're still friends so I picked that club rather than one of the others. My luck

I had to be there on that particular night. But, you know, I go there a lot. Maybe not a lot but I'll drop in now and then."

"Interesting," Haig said. "Mr. Lippa? Can you confirm that?"

Buddy Lippa nodded. "I seen him before," he said. "I dint make him at first but I seen him. Comes in once, twice a week, sits at the bar. Never stays any length of time. And he's right about leaving before Cherry got the needle. I can't swear to the time but I'd guess he came in like nine-thirty and left by ten o'clock. That's not on the dot but it's close."

"Absolutely right," Flatt said. "I was out of there by ten. And I was in a bar on Long Island by midnight, and I can prove that with no trouble whatsoever."

"You needn't," Haig said. "So you've been in the habit of patronizing Treasure Chest once or twice a week. That's interesting."

Flatt didn't say anything.

"There are topless clubs on Long Island, are there not? And are they not more conveniently located, since you both live and work there?"

"Sometimes I'm in New York on business."

"Precisely my point. I submit that your visits to Treasure Chest are a business matter."

"I don't know what you're talking about."

"Nonsense," Haig said. "You know precisely what I am talking about. Five months ago Miss Wolinski went to work at Treasure Chest. You have kept in contact with her and visited the club, perhaps out of curiosity. You needed money, you have always needed money, your gambling habit is such that you shall always need money. And you met someone at Treasure Chest who showed you a way to make all the money that you needed."

"You're out of your mind."

"That's not inconceivable. It is, however, irrelevant to the present discussion. You met someone at Treasure Chest, someone who was regularly present there during the ensuing months. You got into conversation. You mentioned your occupation, and your new acquaintance saw possibilities for profit. You had access, I have mentioned earlier, to poisonous compounds. There is, thanks be to God, no enormous profit at present in such compounds. But you also had access to quantities of a subtler, slower form of poison. As a pharmaceutical chemist, Mr. Flatt, you had access to drugs."

I looked at Flatt. He was keeping a stiff upper lip but the effort was showing. I glanced at Gregorio and saw him nodding thoughtfully. Leonard Danzig had a wary look in his eyes. Gus Leemy was frowning.

"You stole drugs from your employers," Haig was saying. "Perhaps you produced others. I understand lysergic acid can be readily synthesized by anyone with a middling knowledge of chemistry. With your background and your laboratory facilities it would be

child's play. You brought consignments of drugs to
New York, once or twice a week, and you delivered
them to your associate at Treasure Chest—"

"That's horseshit." Gus Leemy was leaning forward, the light glinting off the top of his head. "I run
that place clean. It's not a front for nothing at all. It's a
decent operation."

Gregorio said, "There's drugs coming out of there,
Gus. Been going on for months, the rumbles we get."

"You're crazy." He glanced at Danzig, then averted
his eyes quickly as if remembering that he and Danzig
were supposed to be pretending they didn't know
each other. Since the two of them gave each other an
alibi for Cherry's murder I didn't quite grasp the logic
of this, but they could play it whatever way they
wanted. "I run that place clean," Leemy said. "I don't
fuck with drugs, I never did and I never will."

"I never accused you, sir." Haig tapped his pipe on
the desk again, then frowned suddenly at the bowl
with the two dead goldfish in it. He rang the bell. I
thought that would probably throw Wong, who
wouldn't know what to come in with, but instead
Wong came in empty-handed. Haig nodded at the
bowl and Wong removed it. "I never accused you, Mr.
Leemy," Haig went on. "If you stand accused of anything it is incompetence. Your nightclub served as a fo-
cal point for the dissemination of drugs, but this
occurred without your knowledge. While that does
not make you a particularly efficient manager, neither

does it make you a criminal. It certainly does not make you a murderer." Haig stroked his beard. "Or you, Mr. Danzig. You or Mr. Leemy might well have killed the person selling drugs out of the Treasure Chest, or issued an order that the person be killed, but neither of you would have had any reason to do away with Miss Abramowicz."

Danzig didn't exactly glower but his face hardened a little. "Your reasoning is interesting," he said. "But I'm not sure how my name got in that last sentence. I was going out with Cherry, that's all. That's the only reason I'm here."

"Oh, come off it, Danzig," Gregorio said. He leaned forward and put a hand on Danzig's shoulder. "Everybody knows Leemy just fronts for you. And nobody much gives a shit. The boys from the State Liquor Authority might be unhappy but they can't prove anything, and as far as we're concerned we don't care."

Danzig smiled. "I have no connection with Treasure Chest. Mr. Leemy is a friend."

"Sure, if that's the way you want it."

"That's what the record should show," Danzig said.

All of this was fascinating, but none of it had much to do with who killed Cherry and I was getting impatient. The suspense was fairly thick in the room. I looked at all of them, and the most agitated one was Glenn Flatt, although he wasn't approaching hysteria yet. He should have been the coolest; I mean, he presumably knew who his contact was, and thus he knew who committed the murder.

"I could sue you," Flatt said.

"Oh, come now," Haig said. "You're going to go to jail at the very least for selling illegal drugs and as accessory to the fact of murder in the first degree. Do you really think you could find a lawyer to represent you in a libel action? I somehow doubt it."

"You can't prove any of this."

Haig grunted. "I will tell you something," he said. "There is nothing much simpler than proving something one already knows to be true. The proof generally makes itself available in relatively short order. No, Mr. Flatt, your position is hopeless. You have been selling drugs through a confederate. And what do we know about this accomplice of yours?" He ticked off the points on his fingers. "Your accomplice is regularly to be found at Treasure Chest, either as an employee or an habitual hanger-on. There are several here in this room who fit that description. Miss Wolinski, for one. Mr. Danzig. Mr. Leemy. Mr. Barckover. Miss Remo. Miss Cubbage. Mr. Henderson frequents Treasure Chest often, but if he were selling drugs he would no doubt do so through the medium of one or another of his stores, and—"

"Drugs!" Haskell was outraged. "Me sell drugs? You have to be out of your mind. Drugs are a death trip."

"Indeed. We have already excluded you, Mr. Henderson, so you've no need to offer comments. To continue. Miss O'Connor has not been regularly employed at Treasure Chest, so she too may be ruled out. Mr. Leemy and Mr. Danzig may also be excused; they quite clearly did not know what was going on in the establishment. I would further exclude Mr. Lippa because I find the whole nature of this operation incompatible with my impressions of the man."

"Does that mean I'm in or out?" Buddy wanted to know, and Haig nodded and said that was exactly his point, and that Buddy was in the clear.

"Now let us reconstruct the day of the crime. Mr. Flatt's accomplice in the drug operation—let us call him X, as a sop to tradition—has learned directly or indirectly from Miss Abramowicz that I have been hired to investigate the death of the fish. X realizes that my participation will quickly establish that an attempt has been made on Miss Abramowicz's life and that the fish were unintentional victims. When this became known, Miss Abramowicz would realize that she possesses some information which makes her dangerous to X, and this information would at once be brought to my attention. That, to be sure, was the original motive for disposing of Miss Abramowicz. She somehow learned enough about the drug operation to make her dangerous, especially in view of the fact that she seems to have been rather scatterbrained and loose-tongued. One hesitates to speak thus of the dead, but the fact appears to be beyond dispute.

"Thus X must act, and act quickly. So X contacts Mr. Flatt—yes, sir, it happened just that way, and you needn't attempt to deny it by shaking your head. X contacted you, Mr. Flatt, and demanded a contact poison. Whether curare was specified or not I have no idea. It hardly matters. You had already supplied strychnine to X, although I cannot state with certainty that you knew how it was to be employed. It is often used as an adulterant in drugs to boost their potency and you might well have furnished it without knowing you were to be the instrument in a homicide. But if there is any other use for curare I am unaware of it. You knew Miss Abramowicz was to be killed, sir. You brought the curare that night with that specific purpose in mind. That was why you took pains to leave the club early, why you established an alibi in Long Island. You are a knowing accessory to murder, sir."

Flatt stared at him, and Haig stared back, and Flatt couldn't take it. He looked down at his hands.

"You brought the curare," Haig went on. "You delivered it to X. You left. And X waited, because the last thing X wanted was to murder Miss Abramowicz on the premises of the nightclub. Ideally X would have waited until the evening had come to a close. X and Miss Abramowicz would have left together, and X would have managed to perform the deed in private.

This plan was spiked when Mr. Harrison made an appearance at the club. X learned his identity, realized he was my associate, and recognized that there would be no opportunity to go off with Miss Abramowicz and deal with her as planned. Mr. Harrison would instead be interrogating Miss Abramowicz immediately after she finished her performance, at which time her knowledge might well be passed on to him. And this was something X was wholly unprepared to leave to chance.

"And so X waited, waited until the last minute. Waited until Miss Abramowicz was at the very conclusion of her act, and then injected curare into her bloodstream and killed her."

I saw it all again in slow motion. The finale of the act, Cherry shaking her breasts over the edge of the stage, straightening up, doing her spread, going coyly prim, then trying so desperately to reach her breast—

"When we think of curare," Haig said, "we think of savages in the jungle. We think of blow darts, we think of arrows tipped with the deadly elixir. And when we consider this crime, we assume that X must have employed such a device, that some projectile served to carry curare from X's hand to Miss Abramowicz's breast. No projectile remained stuck in the breast in question; hence we assume that the dart or arrow or whatever struck the breast, pierced the skin, and then fell away. Mr. Harrison was the first person to leap onto the stage after Miss Abramowicz fell. He had the presence of mind, after determining there was no office he could perform for the victim, to make a quick search for the projectile. And he—"

"And he put it in his pocket." This from my old friend Wallace Seidenwall. "I knew Harrison had it. I been saying so all along, and I been saying—"

"You have been saying far too much, sir. Mr. Harrison did not find the projectile. Neither did the police, who may be presumed to have subjected the premises to an exhaustive search. Dismissing such preposterous theories as an arrow with an elastic band tied to it—and I trust we can dismiss such rot out of hand—it is quite inconceivable that X could have retrieved the projectile. Sherlock Holmes established the principle beyond doubt, and I reiterate it here and now: When all impossibilities have been eliminated, that which remains is all that is possible. There was no projectile."

I suppose everybody was supposed to gasp when he said this. That's not what happened. Instead everybody just sat there staring. Maybe they had trouble following what he'd just said. Maybe they were confused about the difference between a weapon and a projectile. I'd already had a lesson in that department so I managed to stay on top of things, and at that moment I finally figured out who X was. Instead of feeling brilliant I sat there wondering how it had taken me so long.

"There was no projectile," Haig said again. "Miss Abramowicz was stabbed with some sort of pin. A hair pin, a hat pin, it scarcely matters. The pin was pressed into her breast and withdrawn. Then—"

"Wait." It was Gregorio. "Unless I'm off-base, she was all alone on that stage. How did someone stick a pin in her breast without anyone seeing it?"

"Because she was bending over the edge of the stage. She did this at the conclusion of every performance, leaning forward almost parallel to the floor with her breasts suspended over the stage apron. This was X's genius—it would have been simpler by far to inflict a wound in her foot, for example, but by waiting for the one perfect moment X could guarantee that everyone would assume that a nonexistent projectile had been employed."

I said, "How come she didn't feel anything? She went right ahead and got up and danced around for a minute, and then there was suddenly blood on her breast and she started to crumble."

"Curare is not instantaneous. Poisons borne by the bloodstream need time to reach the heart. And small puncture wounds rarely begin bleeding immediately. Indeed they often fail to bleed at all. As for her failure to react, she was caught up in an intense dance routine. She might have been too involved to feel a pinprick. She might have assumed it was an insect bite and ignored it. For that matter, she might not have felt it at all. She had had silicone implants. The skin of her breasts was thus stretched to accommodate their enlargement, the nerve endings consequently far apart.

Some nerves may even have been severed when the silicone was implanted."

Haig shrugged. "But it hardly matters. Once one knows how the murder was committed, the identity of X is instantly obvious. Indeed it has been obvious to me for some time that only one person was ideally situated to commit the murder. That same person was also ideally situated to receive consignments of drugs from Mr. Flatt and dispense them in the normal course of occupational routine.

"Miss Remo. I suggest you keep your hands in plain sight and avoid sudden movements. Mr. Wong Fat has you within line of sight. He could plant his cleaver in your head before you could get your purse open. Yes, keep your hands right where they are, Miss Remo. Mr. Seidenwall, I trust you thought to bring a pair of handcuffs? I suggest you put them on Miss Remo. She is rather more dangerous than she looks."

Eighteen

SEIDENWALL PUT THE cuffs on her. He may have been a witling but he knew how to follow orders. I didn't take my eyes off her until the bracelets snapped shut. Then I let out a breath I hadn't remembered taking and glanced at the doorway. Wong was standing there and he still had the cleaver raised. He wasn't taking any chances.

Gregorio lit a cigarette and blew out a lot of smoke. He said, "You don't really have anything, do you? Just a theory. I'm not arguing with your theory. I have to hand it to you, you tied all the ends together and made it work. And if we put the jury in this room and let you put on a show for them they might bring in a conviction, but that's not how the system works. Maybe it should be but it isn't."

"You need proof."

"Right."

"And I told you earlier that proof is the world's cheapest commodity. The contents of Miss Remo's purse might prove interesting. Even if she has been bright enough to avoid bringing anything incriminating with her, you should have little trouble tying her to Flatt and to the drug operation. Once you know what to look for it's a simple matter to find it. You might start by establishing a link between Mr. Flatt and the strychnine in this jar." He tapped the jar of wheat germ. "Odd that this would be left accessible, but perhaps neither of them had an opportunity to retrieve it."

That was all Glenn Flatt needed. He whirled around and glared at Jan Remo. "You stupid ass-faced little bitch! You said you switched jars yesterday afternoon. What in the hell is the matter with you?"

Jan Remo didn't turn a hair. She just closed her eyes for a moment, and when she opened them she spoke in a calm and level voice.

She said, "Now I know why you're such a terrible gambler, Glenn. How many times do you let the same man bluff you out of a pot? There was nothing in that jar of wheat germ. He doctored it with something that would kill the fish." She sighed. "I think it's about time somebody advised me of my rights. I have the right to remain silent. I intend to remain silent. Glenn, I think you should remain silent, too. I really do."

* * *

Gregorio advised them both of their rights and put cuffs on Flatt, and he and Seidenwall led the two of them away. Wong closed the door after them and returned to the kitchen to hang up his cleaver. In the office everybody seemed to be waiting for somebody else to say something. When the silence got unbearable I broke it by asking how he knew Mallard had been killed.

"I don't," he said. "I *believe* he was killed. A police investigation might establish that either Mr. Flatt or Miss Remo was at his apartment yesterday."

"And made him choke on his own vomit?"

Haig nodded slowly. "A simple murder method," he said, "and quite undetectable. It requires a victim who has had a lot to drink. When he has passed out or fallen asleep, one puts one's hand over his mouth and drives one's knee into the pit of his stomach. The victim regurgitates, cannot open his mouth, and the vomit is drawn into the lungs. One might find that Mr. Mallard's abdomen is bruised. This would still prove nothing. It's my guess that Miss Remo killed him, and it's virtually certain that she will never be charged with the crime."

"Nobody could make it stick," Leonard Danzig said.

"Quite so. But both she and Mr. Flatt will serve long sentences for the murder of Miss Abramowicz. Perhaps that is sufficient."

There was some more conversation, and then they left, a few at a time. Leonard Danzig took me aside on his way out and handed me two envelopes. "The other half of what I gave you last night," he said, "plus the bonus we agreed on. All in cash. If Haig wants to pay taxes on it that's his business, but it won't show up on my books so it's strictly up to him. Your boss is everything you said he was. It was worth four grand to watch him operate. It was worth more than that to find out that Gus Leemy hasn't been running as tight a ship as he should. No wonder the police were leaning on me. They thought I had a hand in a drug operation. I don't touch drugs." He smiled. "You're okay yourself. Anytime you drop by the club, there won't be any check."

Within half an hour they were all gone. Maeve O'Connor told me to hang onto her phone number even though the case was solved, and Rita Cubbage gave me her number, too. "In case you want to call me in the middle of the night," she said, "if something should suddenly come up." Simon Barckover asked Haig if he had ever thought of working up a nightclub routine. He started to sketch out what he had in mind but Haig glowered at him and he let it lie. Gus Leemy walked out looking very unhappy and Buddy Lippa trailed after him, looking very stupid. That left our client and her boyfriend, and I got rid of him myself.

I took old Haskell aside and told him he ought to divorce his wife, and he got into a riff about how he couldn't leave her because she would never be able to get another man, so I figured the hell with it and told him how nicely she had done in that department just that morning. This rattled him, and then I told him that I didn't think he should hang around Tulip anymore, and this rattled him a little too, and he went away.

So Tulip was the only one left, and she went home after Haig gave back her check for five hundred dollars. When she refused to take it he tore it up and threw it in the wastebasket.

"But that's not fair," she said. "I hired you to do a job and you did more than I hired you to do and now you won't let me pay you for it."

"I have been amply paid by someone else," he said. "And I am not refusing your payment. I am buying something in return. Use some of that five hundred to buy some good equipment and a group of breeder scats. Select a pair. Breed them. Then tell me exactly how you did it."

Nineteen

WE SPENT PART of the evening Scotch-taping hundred-dollar bills together. This would have been easier if we'd kept them in order but I dropped the second batch and they got all jumbled up. We had to match serial numbers. It didn't really take all that long, but the process kept getting interrupted by people calling from the newspapers and things like that.

Then Haig made me play a few games of chess with him, which I won, and then I played a game with Wong and lost in ten moves. And finally I stood up and said, "I'm going home."

"Very well."

"Oh, hell. You were beautiful today and I can't ruin things by not playing my part. I give up. How did you know to doctor the wheat germ?"

"I gave some of it to some fish while you were seating our guests. They lived to tell the tale." He examined a fingernail. "It was showmanship. I'll admit that. Without it, the police could still turn up enough evidence to convict handily. Addicts who have bought drugs from Miss Remo. Witnesses who could place her and Mr. Flatt in various places at various times." He straightened in his chair. "But I wanted to break them in public. The police dig harder when they know they're digging for something that exists."

"And you got a kick out of the performance."

He grunted.

"So how did you do it? I didn't know we had any strychnine in the house."

"We don't."

"What did you use?"

"Those roach crystals Wong sprinkles around. I dissolved a handful in water and soaked the wheat germ with it."

"How did you know it would kill fish?"

"I didn't. I fed some to some fish and they died."

"I probably should have figured that part out myself. I guess I'm a little punchy. But that's not the main point. How did you *know* they switched jars? How did you know the strychnine was in the wheat germ in the first place?"

He just smiled.

"Oh, hell," I said. "Actually I'm taking some of the credit for this one. Do you remember the pipe dream I was spinning about Haskell Henderson? How he poisoned the fish because Tulip wouldn't eat the health foods but gave them to the fish instead? And how he killed Cherry because she was eating the crap instead of passing it on to Tulip? Remember?"

"That piffle," he said. "How could I possibly forget it?"

"Well, that's what put the idea in your head. And the notion of Jan Remo stabbing Cherry with a pin, you even said hatpin, and you got that idea because I told you how Althea Henderson stuck a hatpin in her tit. For Pete's sake, I'm the one who does all the work around here. Why is it that you get all the credit?"

He petted his beard. "Surely you can make yourself look somewhat more intelligent when you write up this case, Chip. It's only fair that you should have the opportunity."

"Thanks a lot."

"And don't forget what Miss Swann advised you this morning," he went on. "The book needs sex. Not nearly so much as you seem to need it, but it does need sex." He gazed past my shoulder and got a very innocent look on his face. "I see no reason why you couldn't embroider the truth somewhat in that department. In the interest of increasing the book's marketability. You might, oh, fabricate an incident in which you had sexual relations with our client, for example."

I glared at him.

"But that might not be enough in and of itself." He played with his beard some more. "Perhaps you could enlarge this morning's interview with Mrs. Henderson. Suggest that, after she bared her breast to you, you took her to bed. A bit farfetched, to be sure, but perhaps the circumstances warrant it."

Hell.

Was he just guessing? Did he know? Or was he really sincerely suggesting I make up something that he didn't know actually happened?

You tell me. I *still* can't make up my mind.

Be sure to read these other wonderfully funny Chip Harrison mysteries by Lawrence Block . . .

NO SCORE

IT IS A MYSTERY

why a wily, witty, worldly-wise young man-about-town like Chip Harrison has to resort to elaborate arguments and intricate maneuvers to get as beautiful a girl as Francine to go to bed with him.

IT IS A MYSTERY

why a big man with a big gun turns Chip's dream of desire into a nightmare of danger, threatening to make his ultimate moment of bliss the last of his life.

IT IS A MYSTERY

that Chip has to solve fast and furiously, in a sizzling and suspenseful adventure that only Edgar Award–winning Lawrence Block could have written. Chip Harrison rightfully takes his place beside Block's best-known characters.

MAKE OUT WITH MURDER

THE STREETWISE GUMSHOE

is Chip Harrison, who has finally secured himself a job, acting as man-about-town for the corpulent detective Leo Haig. And it's on the dangerous streets of New York that Chip brings home his first case, one in which five beautiful sisters are being systematically murdered by a killer with a diabolical design.

THE UNLUCKY SISTERS

are the Trelawney women, three of whom have already been bumped off, including one who'd stolen Chip's heart. Now he's cozying up to the remaining two, and investigating a couple of other nefarious relatives with motive on their minds.

THE SOLUTION

is a tantalizing, nerve-twisting brainteaser that only Edgar Award–winning author Lawrence Block could have written.

CHIP HARRISON SCORES AGAIN

WHAT MORE CAN A GUY ASK FOR?

ADVENTURE—When young, broke, and girl-less Chip Harrison finds a bus ticket to Bordentown, South Carolina, he knows it was sent by the hand of fate. It's his way out of a wintry, indifferent New York City to a town that sounds downright friendly. . . .

ROMANCE—Bordentown is ready with a warm welcome all right—by the local sheriff. But before long, Chip charms his way into the sheriff's good graces, a job as a bouncer at the local bordello, and the arms of Lucille, the preacher's daughter. . . .

HELP—Even Chip should see he is headed for trouble with a capital T, in another furiously funny caper that could only have been dreamed up by Edgar Award–winning Lawrence Block.

MURDER, MYSTERY AND MAYHEM